M. A. H.

Cosmo's visit to his grandfather

M. A. H.

Cosmo's visit to his grandfather

ISBN/EAN: 9783743355378

Manufactured in Europe, USA, Canada, Australia, Japa

Cover: Foto ©Andreas Hilbeck / pixelio.de

Manufactured and distributed by brebook publishing software (www.brebook.com)

M. A. H.

Cosmo's visit to his grandfather

H.HOLTON.ENG.N.Y.

Cousin's Visit.   Frontispiece.   "She took some clover from my hand, grandpapa."

Page 76.

H. MELTON.

Cosmo's Visit.　　She took her seat on the end of the board.　　Page 123.

COSMO'S VISIT

TO HIS

GRANDFATHER.

BY M. A. H.

AUTHOR OF "GOODLY CEDARS," "THE GLEANERS," ETC.

NEW-YORK:
ROBERT CARTER & BROTHERS,
No. 530 BROADWAY.
1874.

JOHN A. GRAY,
Printer, Stereotyper, and Binder,
16 & 18 Jacob Street, New-York.

CHAPTER I.

"What do you say to trusting Cosmo to go alone, and spend a few weeks with his grandfather this summer?" said Mr. Linton to his wife one morning in July; "he has been studying pretty hard of late, and I think a little freedom from books, and work in the hay-field will do him good. I should like to have him familiar with all the old haunts which I loved so much when I was a boy: the brook where I used to wade and fish, the barn where I used to hunt for eggs, the orchard where I played, and the hill where I used to pick black berries. It almost makes me feel as

1*

if I were a boy again, to think of his enjoying all the sports I used to take pleasure in."

Cosmo's mother looked up from her work,
and smiled at her husband's animation, as
the remembrance of his happy boyhood came
so vividly to his mind, and then she said :

"I am quite as anxious as you that Cosmo should enjoy the country this summer,
but you know I can not leave home, and
he has never been away from me. To be
sure he could go by the boat, and your
father would meet him; he is nine years
old now, and many boys learn to take care
of themselves at that age."

"To be sure they do," said his father,
"and that is one benefit which will arise
from his going, he will learn to depend upon
himself more than he has done, for my
mother can not wait upon him as you do,
though I think she will be glad to have
him come."

"Very well," said Mrs. Linton, "if you

will write to her and ask her, and she is willing to be troubled with a noisy boy about her quiet house, I shall have no objections to letting Cosmo go."

"I will write, then, this afternoon, but we will say nothing to Cosmo about it until the answer comes."

The letter was accordingly sent. Cosmo went on studying his lessons industriously at school, in ignorance of the pleasure in store for him. I am afraid if he had known of it, he would not have been so diligent in preparing for his examination, which was to precede his summer vacation.

Mr. Linton's father owned a large farm, about fifty miles from the city where Cosmo lived. And the large old-fashioned house which his grand-parents occupied, was the same in which his father's childhood had been passed. Cosmo had been in the habit of spending two or three weeks there every summer with his mother. But now Mrs. Linton's mother, who lived with her, was so feeble that she could not leave her, so unless Cosmo went alone, his accustomed visit would have to be given up.

The answer to Mr. Linton's letter came in a few days. "To be sure," said grand-mamma, "let the boy come; I will take as good care of him as I did of you when you were a boy."

Cosmo's father was just reading the letter to his mother, when he ran in with his eyes beaming with delight, and his books in his hand.

"Hurrah!" said he, as he threw them down on the table, "I have done with you for some time at least, and father, I did not miss one word at my examination, and I am to be promoted when school begins again."

"Well done, Cosmo!" exclaimed his father, "I'm glad to hear that; and now, what do you think of going away from these books for a while, to help grandpapa work on his farm?"

"Oh! that would be fine," said Cosmo; "but I thought mother could not leave grandmamma this summer."

"Yes, but a boy who is going to be promoted to a higher class in school, can surely be trusted to go away from home alone," said his father, smiling.

"To be sure, I can go alone; I could take care of my trunk, and I know when the cars get to Norrisville."

"I think the boat will be better; that takes you to Hinton, and there your grandpapa will meet you. But do you think you can take care of yourself after you get there, and not give grandmamma any trouble by inattention to her wishes, or asking her to do for you what you can do just as well for yourself? You can hear what she says about you," continued Mr. Linton, reading from the letter which he still held in his hand: "'If Cosmo has not changed since last summer, he will be no trouble at all; he was then so obedient and desirous of pleasing me, that I loved to have him here.'"

"Dear grandmamma," said Mrs. Linton, her eyes glistening with pleasure at this praise of her boy, "I am sure Cosmo could not do otherwise than obey and love her, for she was all the time thinking of some way to make him happy."

"Yes, indeed," said Cosmo, "didn't she make me nice puddings and pies, though," smacking his lips at the remembrance of them; "and then what a famous swing she made Jerry put up in the old elm tree. I do love her very much."

"Well, my son," said his father, "I hope you will not disappoint her expectations, but try in every way to be obedient and useful. And now what day can mamma have you ready to start?"

"Let me see," said Mrs. Linton, as Cosmo looked eagerly towards her, "this is Friday, I think he can be ready by Wednesday."

"Very well," said Mr. Linton, "I will write to my father then to meet him on Wednesday afternoon. Take care," he continued, laughing, as Cosmo began to caper about the room, " If that is the way you are going off, we shall have to do you up as an express parcel, and label you 'this side up with care.'"

"Oh! I shall be quiet enough when I start," said Cosmo; "this is the way I shall go," and he straightened up with great dignity as he took long strides out of the room to tell Margaret the news.

Margaret had lived in the family ever since Cosmo was a baby, when she used to take care of him. She loved him very much, and he was always sure of an interested listener when he went to tell her any thing. But this time he was disappointed. She shook her head when he told her that he was going off in a boat alone; it was hard for her to realize that the baby which she had nursed so tenderly was able now to take care of himself at all.

"I'm going to help grandpapa 'make hay, too, and ride on horseback," said Cosmo.

"You'll break your neck if you do," said

Margaret. " I wonder what your mother can be thinking of, to let you go; however, if you are going, your clothes must be got ready," and she left Cosmo to go to Mrs. Linton to see what must be done for the boy. While he in his turn went to his room to look over his treasures to see what he should take with him. First, he took from his closet where they were kept, his bag of marbles; but no, he thought, I shall not want those there, for I should have to play alone; I'll take my top, though, for I shall often want to spin that, and my drawing-paper and pencils for rainy days. And as for books, there's the 'Swiss Family Robinson;' I like that and 'Masterman Ready,' and for Sundays there's the 'Pilgrim's Progress;' but no, grandmamma has that. I'll go and ask mamma what I shall take," and off he ran to get his mother to decide the question. She told him that his grandmamma would supply him with Sunday reading, as his father intended sending her some books for that purpose, but he might take the others if he chose.

The days had never passed so slowly in Cosmo's estimation before; they seemed to have twice as many hours as they had ever had before, and it seemed as if Wednesday never would come. One morning passed quickly enough, though, when he went with his father to buy a new fishing-rod, for which he paid his own money, and a new trunk which his father purchased for him, and had his own initials, C. P. L., painted on the end, to Cosmo's great delight.

But when Tuesday came, and he could say, "To-morrow I am going," he was constantly telling the fact to every one as a very important piece of news. He watched Margaret pack his trunk with great interest, and was continually telling her not to forget this thing and that, until she said: "He bothered her so, she didn't know whether she stood on her head or her feet." She liked bustle, though, and this business of preparation had quite reconciled her to Cosmo's going. She even refrained from telling him he would surely be drowned, when he told her that he meant to go fishing in the brook near his grandfather's house, and she entered into the merits of the new fishing-rod with much interest.

The very first rays of the sun, as they peeped into Cosmo's window on Wednesday morning awoke him, and he did not turn over to take another nap and wait for Margaret as he often did, but springing out of bed, exclaiming, "To-day I'm going to grandpapa's," he dressed himself with all possible haste.

"What, my boy, are you up already?" said his father, as his passing through his room awakened him. "This is a good beginning for a farmer's boy, and I must follow your example;" and soon all the household were assembled in the parlor for morning prayers. Cosmo looked a little grave for the first time since his visit to his grandfather had been mentioned, when he saw the shade of sadness on his mother's face, and remembered, that it would be some time before he should see her again.   And when his father prayed "for the child who was to be separated from them for a time," he had a choking sensation in his throat, and he was afraid for a moment that the tears would come, for he thought it would be very unmanly to cry.

I am not sure but he did cry a little, though, when the time came for him to say good-by to his mother, and he clung to her neck so tightly.   But no one saw him if he did, for he ran right out to the carriage, and by the time his father joined him there the tears all disappeared.

They were just driving off when Margaret came running to the door calling to them to stop.   She came to the carriage-window with Cosmo's luncheon-basket in her hand.   "Here Cosmo," said she; "I have put up some cakes for you to eat on the boat, for you did not eat any breakfast, boys never do when they are going away, and you'll be hungry before dinner time." Cosmo hesitated about taking the basket, he was afraid it might look babyish to carry cakes to eat. But his father told him to take it, he might need it before he left the boat. So thanking Margaret, he took the luncheon-basket and deposited it on the seat by his over-coat, and they drove off.

Just as they stepped on board the boat, they met the captain, and Cosmo's father introduced him as a young gentleman going to travel alone for the first time, and who would be glad to have the captain take a little oversight of him.

"That I will, my boy, gladly," said the kind-hearted captain, shaking him by the hand; "for the sake of your father, whom I have known ever since he was your size." They could not stop longer to talk to him then, for just before a boat starts is a busy time for the captain, so Mr. Linton took

Cosmo to the upper deck, and as some minutes would elapse before the boat would start, he sat down by him to watch the vessels which were passing up and down. They had scarcely taken their seats when Cosmo noticed a little girl seated near them with a lady who he supposed was her mother. His attention was attracted by hearing her say: "Oh! dear, why don't the boat go; I'm tired of waiting."

"In a few moments, my dear, the boat will start," was the lady's reply.

"I wish it would start now," said the little girl in the same fretful tone; "I don't like to sit still."

"We will walk around the boat a little then," said the lady, and she took the child's hand and they walked off together.

"That little girl," said Mr. Linton, as soon as they were out of hearing, "has yet to learn the way to travel comfortably."

"What is that, father?" said Cosmo.

"Why it is to be quiet, and contented,

and cheerful, no matter what annoyances may arise. There are many things which we would like to have different from what they are when we travel, but we can not help them, so there is no use in fretting about them, and the less we think about them the better; but there's the last bell, and I must go, let me here from you soon, good by;" and in a moment Cosmo was left standing by himself on the deck. He hastened towards the side next the wharf, and saw his father just stepping from the boat. He stood there to watch it push off, and as it left the wharf, Cosmo waved his hat for farewell.

CHAPTER II.

It was a cool day for the season, and Cosmo enjoyed the sail very much. They soon left the city behind them, and then came the beautiful country-seats, with lawns sloping to the water's edge, where children stopped their play to see the boat go by, and wave their handkerchiefs to the passengers, and Cosmo waved his in return. Sometimes the boat passed high rocks and thick groves of trees, which made Cosmo think of the time when this country was all a wilderness, and he almost fancied that he saw an Indian every now and then, peeping from behind the rocks with his bow and arrow ready to take aim at any skiff which might be passing, just as the early settlers used to see the red men, when they sailed on these waters. But Cosmo's thoughts were

soon recalled to the present time, by hearing
a voice near him say, as he leaned against
the railing of the boat: "Take care, little
boy, you'll lose your hat." For a moment
he felt quite indignant that any one should
think that he, Cosmo Linton, who had been
trusted to take care of himself and his new
trunk, could not take care of his hat.

But when he turned to look at the speaker
he could not feel angry any more. She was
a kind, motherly-looking old lady, and reminded him of his grandmother. She had
a gray stocking in her hand which she was
knitting, and it looked just like the knitting-
work which his grandmother always had
lying on her table ready to take up at any
time. This made him reply rather more
politely than he was at first tempted to do.

"I don't think my hat will be lost, for
this string fastens it," and he pointed to the
string which was tied to his button-hole.

"Dear me, what a good contrivance that
is; I must tell Johnny of that," said the

old lady. "Johnny is my grandson," she continued. "He is a good deal larger than you, though." Then followed a long string of questions—how old was he? where was he going? who was with him, etc. Just such questions as elderly ladies think they can ask every child they meet, and which I hope you will always answer as respectfully as Cosmo did, even if you do not like them any better than he did. But he had been taught always to show respect to age, and he did not forget his teachings then, even though he was trying to think of some way to escape from the old lady.

But when she drew from her pocket a large cake, and asked him " if he would not like a cookie," he could hardly refuse politely.

To think that before all the passengers, he should be treated like such a baby. And when she urged him : " What, not take any ; why, even Johnny likes a cookie; come, don't be bashful, take it," he could hardly

refrain from telling her that he wished
Johnny had it then. Fortunately the clerk
came to his relief. "Ticket, madam," said
he, as he stood by her with one hand full of
bills and the other with tickets, and while
she was feeling for her ticket in the same
capacious pocket from which she had ex-
tracted the "cookie," Cosmo made his escape to the other side of the boat, where he
gave his ticket to the clerk, when he came
to that side.

The boat made several landings before it
reached Hinton, where Cosmo was going to
stop, and they were just approaching one
now. Cosmo watched the men with much
interest as they got the ropes ready to throw
ashore.

The little girl whom he had seen when he
first came on board was seated near him
with her mother, and he heard her say: "Is
that the place we are going to stop at?"

"No!" said her mother," we don't leave
the boat yet for an hour."

"O dear!" said the child. "I wish we were there now, I am so tired of this boat."

"I'm sure there is plenty to see," said her mother. "Look at this pretty place where we are going to land." Just then the boat turned and they were in the sun. "Oh! how hot it is," said the little girl; "I wish the sun would not come on us."

"Put up your parasol," said the lady; "we shall turn again in a few minutes."

"Oh! it's so troublesome to hold," was the fretful reply.

The boat landed, and Cosmo saw to his great joy the old lady walk off on the shore, with the "cookie," he fervently hoped, safe in her pocket."

She was met by a boy a good deal larger than himself, whom Cosmo concluded was "Johnny." He took her bandbox and basket from her in a very respectful manner, and carried them for her as they walked up the hill together.

There was a quantity of freight to land,

and the boat stopped there some time, much
to the annoyance of Mary, for that was the
name which Cosmo heard the lady call the
fretful girl. It was every minute, " Why don't
we start?" " I wish we would go," "I'm tired
of staying here," until her mother took no
notice of her, but let her fret as much as she
wished. At last the boat started and they
were again in the shade, and Cosmo
thought that Mary would surely be satisfied
then ; but no, she wanted a drink. Her
mother told her that there was some in the
cabin.

"Oh ! that's too warm—besides, I don't
like it."

Then a gentleman came and placed his
chair near her, and she did not like to be
crowded. Then she wanted her dinner, and
there was an almost incessant string of com-
plaints until they reached the next landing,
when she left the boat.

You may think because she was a little
girl therefore she was soon tired, but a great

many little children travel without fretting; and if you give way to a discontented spirit when you are young, you will be very apt to be discontented when you grow up. On this lovely day when Mary was sailing up that river, there were the same beautiful things to engage her attention as there were for Cosmo to see. But as she paid no regard to them and only thought of the discomforts, she did not enjoy the sail at all, while he was very happy.

So it is in life. Our Heavenly Father has given us many blessings and much to make us happy, and though there are many things we would like to have changed, let us try not to think of those, but be happy and thankful for the good things he has given us.

Cosmo felt very much elated that the captain had not come to look after him at all, for he thought that proved that he considered him able to take care of himself. But the truth was that the captain had noticed Cosmo's crestfallen expression, as his father

had asked him to take care of him, and as
he knew that he was perfectly safe so long
as he staid on the boat, he had purposely left
him to himself, only taking care that he did
not go on shore at the wrong landing. But
now as the next place would be Hinton, he
thought it was time to have a little chat with
the boy. He found him in a retired corner
where he had gone to eat some of Margaret's
cake unobserved, and he was a good deal
chagrined that the captain should surprise
him just as he was in the act of eating a
large piece of cake, for he was particularly
desirous of appearing manly in his eyes.
But the captain's free and easy manner re-
assured him as he took a seat beside him,
and helped himself to a piece from his
basket, and he began to think it might not
be so babyish after all to eat cake on board
of a boat when one is hungry.

Then the captain began to tell some won-
derful stories about a very knowing dog
which he had, which amused Cosmo greatly,

and drew a crowd of passengers around to listen to him. He was so much interested with these stories that he did not observe that they had approached near enough to the town to see the church steeples until the captain starting up exclaimed: " Here we are almost to Hinton, and I have something else to do besides sitting here to talk ; but come to my house some day, master Cosmo, and my dog will show you himself how much he knows."

As the captain hastened off, Cosmo stationed himself by the railing of the boat to look out for his grandfather. Presently as the boat approached the wharf, he spied him standing there amidst the crowd assembled to see the boat land.

Forgetting for a moment that there was no one to share his delight, he exclaimed aloud, " There he is, there's my grandfather, with his whip in his hand;" and then remembering that he was among strangers, he colored with confusion, while some of the passengers smiled at the eagerness of the boy.

As this was the last stopping-place for the boat, Cosmo remained on deck, as his father had told him to do, until most of the passengers left the boat; for Mr. Linton said, "It was very foolish to push and crowd off the boat, as if every one were trying to be first on shore, and a boy like him would very likely be pushed off the plank if he attempted it." So after the boat landed, Cosmo remained standing where he was until he saw his grandfather coming on board, and then he hastened down-stairs to meet him.

"Ah! my boy," he exclaimed, as Cosmo caught him by the hand; "here you are; I am glad to see you. How you have grown, to be sure; but show me which is your trunk, and then we will be off for home, for your grandmother will not like to have her dinner spoiled."

The trunk was soon found, and carried

to Mr. Linton's wagon; and Cosmo jumping in by the side of his grandfather, the horses trotted off towards home, as fast as if they knew that dinner was waiting for them too.

"Well, Cosmo," said his grandfather, "so you have come to learn to be a farmer this summer."

"Yes, sir," said Cosmo, "my father said he thought you would let me help you."

"That I will, my boy; you may rake hay just as much as you please, and you must learn to drive too—why, you may as well begin now, here's a level piece of road," and putting the reins in Cosmo's hands, his grandfather folded his arms, and leaned back saying, "He was going to be a gentleman now." Cosmo was greatly delighted at this, and he was so busy watching the horses, and attending to his grandfather's directions, about turning out for the wagons they met, that he had no time to ask the numerous questions he had intended to about the chickens and the calves, and the colt.

3*

Cosmo drove all the way to his grandfather's house, without any accident, except once he nearly went into the ditch by the side of the road, in turning out too far for a load of hay.

His grandmother saw them as they drove in the gate, and came to the door to meet them.

She seemed very glad to see Cosmo, and kissed him over and over again. She admired the new trunk, too, very much, and telling Jerry to carry it up-stairs she led Cosmo up to see his room. It was the same one which his father had occupied when he was a boy, right next to his grandmamma's own room. It had not been used for a sleeping-room for some time, but now it had been fitted up expressly for Cosmo with new furniture. The only old piece of furniture was his father's desk, which still stood in the corner just as he used to have it with the three swinging shelves over it for his books.

"Oh! thank you, thank you, grand-mamma," said Cosmo, as he ran up to her and kissed her again, "for giving me this nice room; and what pretty furniture it has! I shall try to keep it always looking as neatly as it does now."

"I am glad to hear you say that," said his grandmamma, pleased at his delight, "and now get ready for dinner, for the bell will ring in a few minutes, and you must be hungry."

Cosmo proved that her words were true, by the alacrity with which he obeyed the summons to dinner when it came, though he was in such a hurry to look about him, that he could hardly be induced to wait for his favorite pudding.

"Now, grandpapa, may I go with you?" said Cosmo, as his grandfather pushed his chair from the table, and took his hat to go out.

"Yes, come along, I am going to see if the meadow just across the brook is not ready for mowing."

So he ran for his hat, and they started off together. They walked along the road for a little while till they came to a lot, where there were four little calves feeding.

"O grandpapa!" exclaimed Cosmo, as he spied them, "what little beauties, may I go and see them?"

"Yes," said his grandfather, "let us go in the lot, but quietly, for they are timid little creatures, and will run away from you, if you are not careful." "Which do you think is the prettiest?" he continued, as they walked up to the place where the calves were feeding. One of them was white, except a brown spot something like a star on its forehead, another was nearly black, another a dark brown, and the fourth brown with a few white spots. Cosmo, stood still a few moments to consider before he answered such an important question, and then said.

"Oh! the white one, grandpapa, with a star on its forehead."

"Well, Cosmo, you may have her for

your own, and when she is grown up to be a cow, you may drink all the milk she gives if you can."

"Why, grandpapa," exclaimed the delighted boy, "are you in earnest, is she my own, how very kind you are, and may I take her home with me?"

"Why, yes, you may take her home if you wish, only I think that she will not like your little yard as well as one of these broad lots, or my comfortable barn."

"No, that's true," said Cosmo, looking a little serious; "well then, if you will take care of her I will leave her here when I go, but then I may feed her while I am here, may I not?"

"Certainly, I expect that you will take all the care of her while you are here."

"Then I'll feed her now," exclaimed Cosmo, as he pulled up some grass and went towards her, calling, "Here Bossy, here Bossy," as he remembered to have heard his grandfather call the calves, when he was there last summer.   But Bossy did not understand his kind intentions, and only raised her head and looked at him until he came quite close to her, and then bounded away to the other side of the field.   "Never mind," said his grandfather, as he saw Cosmo's disappointed look, "she'll be tamer after awhile; come with me now to the meadow, and you can pick some clover for her."

So they went on over the clear brook, which they crossed by stepping-stones, and then Mr. Linton let down some bars, and they were in a beautiful field of clover. "Yes," said he looking around, "I think I shall mow this to-morrow."

"O grandpapa! may I help you?"

"Why, you are rather too small to handle a scythe yet, but you may rake and toss it after it is mown, if you like, but now don't forget to gather some clover for your calf."

Cosmo picked a large bunch of it, and then they recrossed the brook, and came into the field where the calves were. His white calf was quietly feeding again, but this time he did not go close up to her—he only laid some of the clover near her, and then walked away a few steps. She smelt the fragrant blossoms, and then ate them up, looking about for more. Cosmo scattered some more on the ground nearer to him, and she cautiously came towards it. When that was eaten, and she again raised her head for more, Cosmo held out what he had in his hand, and stood very still. Bossy looked for a minute as if she was half-afraid to come, but the clover was very good, and looked very tempting, so she came along slowly, and timidly took it from Cosmo's hand. He was so delighted that he could hardly wait for her to eat it, he was so impatient to go to tell his grandfather who was still standing by the brook. But as soon as the calf had finished she seemed to understand that there was no more, and bounded away again as before. Cosmo ran to his grandfather, exclaiming:

"She took some clover from my hand, grandpapa."

"Oh! then you'll soon make her very tame, and she will learn to know you too, but what are you going to call her?"

"Why that is what I can't decide upon. I suppose 'Star' would be a good name, because she has that brown mark like a star on her forehead; but I don't think it would be a nice name to call," and Cosmo began to call "Star! Star!" to see how it would sound. But he shook his head, that did not suit him.

"How do you like Whitey?" said his grandfather."

"Oh! I don't think that is a pretty name; besides, one of your cows has that name. I might call her Friskie, for she frisks about so, only that would not do so well for her when she is a sober old cow. Would White-foot do? To be sure she is white all over, but then her feet are white too, and I like the sound of the name," and he began repeating

over "White-foot! White-foot!" just as he
said Star before, only he seemed to like this
the best.

His grandfather thought it a very good
name, and that her being all white did not
make any difference. So Cosmo decided that
White-foot should be the name of his new
pet, and he hastened home to tell his grandmother about it.

He found her just going out to see after
her chickens; so he followed her with the
meal and corn to feed them, telling her as he
went all about his pretty calf, and the name
he had chosen. His grandmother was very
much interested, and said she hoped that
Whitefoot would give as much milk by and
by, as her mother Whitey did.

"Why, is Whitey her mother? How odd
that I should have chosen a name for her so
like her mother's!" said Cosmo.

The hens all came fluttering around Mrs.
Linton as they saw her coming, and the
roosters stalked majestically up, as if they

were conscious that they were strong enough to get what they wanted without being in such a hurry as the silly hens were. However, to do them justice, they did call the hens to come too, and even picked up some grains of corn and laid them at their feet. Cosmo gave the little chickens, who were still in the coops with their mothers, their supper of meal and water, and he was very much amused to watch them. One little thing not only ate all she could find on the ground, but picked off from her mother's bill all the meal that had stuck to that, and after they had had their supper and the old hen called them to come under her wings and go to sleep, a little black chicken was so impudent as to climb on his mother's back, instead of going to bed.

After the chickens were fed, Cosmo went to see the cows milked, and then the tea-bell rang, and after supper he was so tired that he was glad to go to bed, particularly as his grandfather told him, that farmers must get up very early in the morning.

CHAPTER III.

The next morning the first rays of the sun as they peeped through the vines which shaded Cosmo's window, awoke him, and instantly he recollected that to-day he was going to begin to be a farmer, and he must get up early, so he sprang out of bed and began to dress himself very fast indeed. As he went to his neatly packed trunk to get the clothes which he needed for the day, he was reminded of his mother and her thoughtful care for him, and he wished that he could see her and kiss her for good-morning, particularly when he saw his Bible and prayer-book which she had placed there. Then he remembered how she had told him never to forget in the morning to thank his Heavenly Father for his care over him through the night, and to ask Him to watch over him, and keep him from evil and sin through the day. So as soon as he was dressed he found the place in his little Bible where he had been reading every day with his mother, and after reading a chapter, knelt down and offered his morning prayer. He felt almost as if he had seen his father and mother after praying to God to take care of them and bless them.

As early as Cosmo arose, his grandfather was up before him, and just as he was leaving his room he heard his voice under his window calling him to get up. He ran down-stairs exclaiming: "I'm up, grandpapa, and all dressed too."

"Well done, my boy," said his grand father, as Cosmo came running towards him, "this is a very good commencement for a farmer, and now let us have prayers and then breakfast before we go to work, for it is an old and true saying that 'prayers and provender hinder no man's journey;' so the bell was rung, and the family assembled for worship. There was Cosmo and his grand-

parents, and Jerry, the boy who lived there
and did the little odds and ends to be done
about a farm, which the farmers call chores,
and Abby and Sophy, who did the work
of the house. Cosmo listened very atten-
tively as his grandfather read, and when he
prayed for his parents, and for him, that he
might be a comfort to them, the tears came
into his eyes as he thought it would be some
time before he should see them again.

However, he could not miss his parents
much while his grandparents were so kind,
and all thoughts of home were banished from
his mind, when at breakfast his grandfather
proposed that he should take his new fishing-
rod and try to catch some fish for dinner, in
the brook near the meadow which he intended to mow that day; "because," he continued, "you know, Cosmo, that the grass
must dry a little after it is cut before we
begin to toss and rake it for hay."

Cosmo was very willing to try his new
fishing-pole, so off he ran up-stairs to get it.

As he returned with it in his hand, he said. "You know, grandpa, I shall want to feed Whitefoot on my way to the brook."

"To be sure, and I dare say your grandma will give you some salt for her, and you may come and get some clover from the meadow while I am mowing."

His grandmamma gave him a cup full of salt, and with this and his new fishing-rod he started off with his grandfather. The calves were in the same field in which they were the day before, and Cosmo stopped a moment to admire them, but he wanted to get Whitefoot some clover before he gave her the salt. So he followed his grandfather on to the hayfield. One of the men was already at work there mowing. Mr. Linton threw off his coat and took the other scythe which was there, to work also.

"I wish I could mow," said Cosmo, as he watched the grass fall before the scythe, and lie in regular rows; "it looks very easy."

"Yes, easy to them that knows how," said

Caleb, the man who was mowing, and who happened to hear Cosmo, "but not to those who don't. Why, I knew a little chap once who, like you, thought it easy enough, and took up a scythe one day to try, but he nearly cut his leg off."

"Why, how?" said Cosmo.

"Why, you see a scythe is the most un-manageable thing if you don't know how to use it, and as he swung it round hard it came quickly through the grass and against his leg, and before he knew it, the blood was streaming."

"How dreadful!" said Cosmo; "but did he get well?"

"Ah! that he did, and learned to mow well after that, as you can see for yourself," said Caleb, as he gave a vigorous stroke with the scythe.

"Why, were you that boy?" said Cosmo.

"Well, I was, and I have the scar in my leg yet to remind me never to think I can do any thing without being taught how."

Just then Cosmo's grandfather called to him not to forget his calf, so taking an armfull of the sweet clover which Caleb had cut down, and his cup of salt, and leaving his fishing-pole by the fence, he went back again to the field where the calves were.

He called, "Whitefoot! Whitefoot!" saying to himself: "She may as well become accustomed to her name at once." She was in a corner of the field by herself, and as Cosmo called she raised her head and stood still for a moment; he approached nearer and nearer to her, and when he was close enough he threw her some salt; she licked it up and then looked for more. He threw her some, going a little nearer, and then sprinkling it along the ground to the place where he stood. Whitefoot came on, licking up the salt until she came quite close to him, and then he held out some of the clover for her to eat. She took it from his hand quite graciously, and as she was eating Cosmo ventured to stroke her head. She seemed rather surprised at the liberty, but she liked the clover too well to go away, so she remained still, eating.

Cosmo was quite delighted. "Now," thought he, "if grandpapa will only let me keep her away from the rest, and near the house, I know she will become quite tame very soon."

So as soon as the clover was all eaten up, Cosmo hastened back to the field to ask his grandfather about it.

"I have no objection," said Mr. Linton. "We will take her when we go to dinner; but I thought you were going to catch me some fish."

"Oh! so I am, and here's my new fishing-pole by the fence."

It was one of those poles which are formed of several pieces, and when Cosmo had fastened them together, and adjusted his line and hook, as his father had told him how, he carried it to show it to Caleb. Caleb admired it very much, "but," said he, "you have no bait; how are you going to catch any fish ?"

"Oh! I forgot the bait," said Cosmo, as he ran off to his grandfather to ask him what he should do. Mr. Linton smiled as he said: "I noticed that you had no bait, but I preferred to let you find it out for yourself, for you will be less likely to forget what you want the next time. Now, if you go back to the house, you will probably find Jerry in the garden picking vegetables; you can ask him to dig you some worms for bait, and then bring them to me, and I will show you how to put them on your hook; but stop a minute," he continued, as Cosmo started to run off, "think of every thing you want before you come back."

Cosmo stopped and thought.

"I suppose I ought to have a basket to put my fish in."

"Yes," said his grandfather.

"And something to hold my bait, and a knife, and then I should like a drink from

that spring in the meadow, so I'll ask grandmamma to let me have a tin cup, and ——
I guess that's all," he concluded, as he started
again.

He found Jerry in the garden, and he
readily agreed to dig his bait for him while
he went to ask his grandmother for something to put it in. She gave him an old tin
pan for his bait, and also a basket, a tin cup,
and a knife which he asked her for. Then
he went to Jerry, and found him in a corner
of the garden digging.

"There's bait enough to catch twenty
fishes," said Jerry, as he put the worms in
Cosmo's tin pan; "only I don't believe you'll
catch so many."

"What's the reason, I'd like to know?"
said Cosmo.

"Oh! because you'll soon get tired."

Cosmo did not like this very well; he
thought Jerry was making fun of him, and
did not think he was as old as he considered
himself to be. However, he said nothing,

but thought, "I'll show Jerry he's mistaken," as he went out of the gate, with his basket containing his tin cup and knife in one hand, and his pan of bait in the other. The sun was very hot, and as Cosmo went along he was a little inclined to be out of humor with his grandfather for not reminding him of these things before he left home, and saving him this hot walk.

"I'm sure mamma would not have done so," he thought. The truth was, that Cosmo had been used to having his mother and Margaret remind him of every thing he needed. When he was going to school they got him his luncheon and books, and wherever he was going, they said to him: "Don't forget this or that, Cosmo." So he had never learned to depend upon himself at all, and that was what his grandfather wanted to teach him.

However, grumbling did no good, and he soon forgot both the heat and the ill-humor when he reached the cool shady brook. His

Cosmo's Visit.   He rebaited his hook.   P. 49.

grandfather was waiting for him there, to show him how to bait his hook; but first, he led him to a part of the brook, some distance from the stepping-stones, where the water was deeper, and the shade thicker. There seated on a large stone under a tree, his grandfather left him. It was very pleasant to sit there in the shade, for Cosmo was tired. Pretty soon his cork bobbed down, he drew his line in quickly, and there was a little fish hanging on the end of it. He took it off, and re-baited his hook, and in a few minutes he caught another, and then another, until he had caught five in a very short time. Then a good while elapsed and he had not a bite, and he had just said to himself, "There's no use in trying any more," when he remembered what Jerry had said about getting tired, and he determined to try again. This time he was more successful, and by the time his grandfather came to see how he was getting on, he had caught ten.

"That's enough for one morning, my boy,"

said Mr. Linton as Cosmo showed them to him triumphantly; "we will take them home now to be fried for dinner. I am going to leave the rest of the field for Caleb, for I want to go to the mill this afternoon, and you can go with me."

Cosmo hastily put up his fishing-rod and prepared to go home, for he thought, " Perhaps grandpapa will let me drive a little."

" I guess we'll leave Whitefoot here till to-morrow, grandpapa," said Cosmo, as they passed through the field together. His grandfather made no objection, so they went straight home.

Cosmo met Jerry at the kitchen-door, and he showed him his fish quite triumphantly : "You see I did catch a good many, and I would have caught more, only my grandfather said that it was time to come home."

" Well," said Jerry, " now I suppose you want me to clean them." So laying down the armfull of wood which he had brought for the kitchen fire, he took the fish to a bench just outside of the kitchen-door, and proceeded to prepare them for cooking.

Cosmo watched him until the bell rang for dinner. He did not want to go without his fish, but Sophy told him that she would soon cook them and send them in. So Cosmo ran into the dining-room, and his grandfather looked pleased, for he liked to have all his family punctual at their meals.

Pretty soon, Susan brought in the fish smoking hot, and Cosmo's grandfather and grandmother praised them very much, and as for Cosmo himself, he thought he had never tasted such nice fish before.

CHAPTER IV

After dinner Cosmo went to the barn to see Jerry harness the horses. "I wish you would let me help you," said he as he stood there watching Jerry; "it seems very easy."

"Well," replied Jerry; "just put this collar on Bessie, then," handing the collar to him.

Bessie was very gentle, and stood very still while Cosmo, standing on tip-toe, tried to put the collar over her head. He knew which was the top, and he supposed that of course, that must go on over the horse's ears, so he pushed and pushed in vain; he could not get it on. "See here, Jerry," said he at last, his patience exhausted. "This can't be Bessie's collar, it is too small for her."

"Oh! yes, it is hers, and it an't too small, either, only you don't know how to put it on." Then Jerry came round to him and showed him that the collar was larger at the bottom than at the top, and so he must put it on upside down, and then turn it after it was on.

Cosmo felt a little mortified that he had showed so much self-confidence again that day, and he silently watched Jerry finish harnessing the horse. The truth was, that one of Cosmo's greatest faults was thinking that he knew more than he did, and he was constantly attempting to do things which he had never been taught to do, and consequently was often mortified at failures.

Jerry had scarcely got the horses into the wagon, when Mr. Linton came out to the barn. He helped Jerry lift some bags of corn into the wagon, and then put an empty bag in for chicken-feed, which he said he meant to get at the mill. Cosmo noticed that his grandfather seemed to think of every thing that he might need, and he thought of his own forgetfulness that morning, and the trouble it had cost him, and he determined to think next time too.

At last his grandfather was ready, and Cosmo jumped into the wagon beside him, and off they drove. As soon as they were out into the road Mr. Linton gave Cosmo the reins, saying: "Now we'll see how you can drive."

He took them eagerly, but he had learned a lesson from his self-confidence that afternoon, so he was unusually attentive in following his grandfather's directions, and he drove all the way to the lane which led to the mill.

Here his grandfather took the reins, for the lane was a narrow one, and if they should meet a wagon, it would not be so easy to turn out for it. There was a very steep bank sloping from the road on one side, at the foot of which ran a clear stream, which Cosmo could see through the trees, dancing gayly along in the sunlight. On the other side of the road a hill rose above them,

Cosmo's Visit   "O grandpapa! what a beautiful place."   Page 63.

covered with rocks and trees, and bushes. It was a very romantic, pretty place, and Cosmo was delighted. "O grandpapa!" he exclaimed; "what a beautiful place. I should like to live here always." But when they descended the hill he was more charmed still. There stood the mill by the side of the stream, completely shut in by hills and tall trees, and the splashing of the wheel as it turned was the only sound or sign of life there.

A man came to the door as Mr. Linton drove up. He was the miller, and Mr. Linton asked him if he could grind his corn that afternoon, adding that he was going farther on to the village, but he would leave the grain until he came back. The miller said he could grind it at once, and proceeded to take the bags out of the wagon. Cosmo's grandfather gave him his choice, to stay and see the corn ground, or to go with him.

"I would rather stay, if you please, grandpapa," said Cosmo.

"Very well, I will be back in less than an hour, but be careful not to go too near the wheel," said he, as he drove off.

Cosmo followed Mr. Ford, for that was the miller's name, into the mill, and watched him as he emptied the corn into the hopper. Then he saw it crushed between the two great stones, and fall into the great sieve below, where it was thrown out, fine meal on one side, and on the other something which Cosmo recognized as the same which his grandmother used to feed her chickens. After he had watched the corn grinding for some time, he went outside of the mill and strolled along by the side of the stream, amusing himself by throwing stones into the water and trying to make them skip.

He had thrown a large stone into the water, and was enjoying the noise it made, when some one called out:

"Hallo! don't do that, you'll frighten all the fish away," and looking over to the other side of the stream, he saw a boy a little larger than himself, seated on a stone, fishing.

"Oh! I didn't see you before," said Cosmo. "Have you caught any fish?"

"Oh! yes, a good many," said the boy; "but I can't catch any more if you go on throwing stones."

"Can I come over there?" screamed Cosmo.

. "Yes, if you can walk a log."

"Where is the log?"

"Just down there."

And looking down the stream, Cosmo saw a log thrown over to the opposite bank. It was rather narrow, to be sure, but some of the branches had been left upon it, and any one trying to cross it, could steady himself by taking hold of these. So he concluded to try it. He crossed safely, and was soon standing by the boy who was fishing. He was a very good-natured boy, and told Cosmo that his name was James Ford, and that it was his father who kept the mill. He said he lived not far from there, and that he would like Cosmo to come to see him some day.

"But how did you know my name?" said Cosmo.

"Oh! I saw you drive along with your grandfather, and Jerry told me last week that you were coming to stay with Mr. Linton. If you'll come some day, we'll make a fire in the woods, and roast corn and potatoes."

"Oh! I should like that," said Cosmo; "I will ask my grandfather if I may; there he comes, I will ask him now."

"I'll go with you," said James. "I've caught fish enough for one afternoon." So taking his string of fish and his pole, he crossed the log with Cosmo. Mr. Linton reached the mill before them, and was talking to Mr Ford as they came up.

He shook James kindly by the hand, as he said: "So my boy has found you out, and has been making friends with you. I hope he will always choose his friends as well." James and his father looked very much pleased—and Cosmo said: "He wants me to come here and spend the day with him some time, and roast corn and potatoes in the woods."

"Well, we will see about that," said his grandfather. "I think James must come to see you first. But now the meal is ground and we must start for home." The bags were soon put into the wagon. Cosmo being quite delighted because he was allowed to help, and still more so when his grandfather put the reins in his hands, and told him that he might drive home all the way. He felt proud that James could see how well he could drive. So proud that he forgot to turn out for a great stone on the side of the road; so the wheels went over it, tipping the wagon all on one side. "Take care," said his grandfather; "if you are not more careful, we will not get home without some accident.

Cosmo's pride was a good deal jolted out out of him by this mishap. So he was more careful after this, and they reached home safely.

The next morning, after breakfast, Cosmo started to go with his grandfather to the hay-field.

"Stop a minute," said Mr. Linton, as they were passing the barn.

Cosmo waited while his grandfather went in the barn, and in a moment came out again with a rake in his hand, just like those Cosmo had seen the hay-makers use, only much smaller.

"I thought you would not be able to manage one of the large rakes which the men use, so I bought this for you yesterday, at the village," said Mr. Linton, as he gave it to Cosmo.

"Oh! thank you, grandpapa," said the little boy very much pleased. "But how did you bring it home; I did not see it in the wagon."

"No, I was very careful to hide it under the bags of meal, so that you should not see it; I wanted to surprise you."

Cosmo shouldered his rake and walked along quite proudly by his grandfather. He was in such haste to try his new rake that he did not wait to feed White-foot, though she came running towards him as he entered the field.

"By and by, White-foot, I'll bring you some clover," said he; "I'm going to make hay now."

They found the men at work when they reached the field. Cosmo watched his grandfather, as he took off his coat and hung it on a tree at the side of the field, and following his example, took off his jacket also, and hung it on the same tree. Then he began to rake the sweet-smelling hay as he saw the others do. His little rake worked very nicely, and he was soon as expert in using it as his grandfather was in using his long-handled one. He was very happy and contented, thinking it great fun to rake hay, when he saw Jerry in one corner of the field working too. "Ah!" thought he; "I will go and show Jerry my rake." So running across the field he called out:

"Look, Jerry; see what a nice little rake my grandfather has bought for me, and see how well I can use it too;" and he began to rake the hay vigorously. Now Jerry loved to tease, a very unkind habit by the way, making those who are teased feel very uncomfortable, to say the least, merely to gratify, for a moment, the one who has it in his power to tease. I think one reason that so many boys and girls love to indulge in this practice is, that they think it makes them seem superior to those whom they tease, and thus they gratify a very contemptible kind of pride. For we always find that it is the stronger who try to tease the weaker, and is not that very cowardly?

But to return to Jerry, as he looked at Cosmo raking, he said:

"Pooh! any one can rake with such a baby thing as that; if you could use one of these that the men use, you might boast— see here." And he used his rake as vigorously as Cosmo had done before him.

Poor Cosmo, his pleasure in his grandfather's present was all gone; but his anger was roused too.

"My rake is not a baby thing," said he, angrily. "My grandfather gave it to me, and if you say so again I'll tell him."

"Yes, do tell," said Jerry; "and then you will be a baby, for babies always tell. But what can we expect of a boy who puts a horse's collar on upside down, ha, ha!" And Jerry began to laugh in a most contemptuous manner. Cosmo could not endure it any longer, and he ran off for fear Jerry should see him cry from vexation, and then he might have some reason for calling him a baby. He went back to the place where he had left his grandfather, but he had gone to another part of the field to speak to one

of the men. His rake was lying on the
ground, and Cosmo took it up saying: "I
don't see why I can't use a large rake too."
But it was very heavy, and it tired his arms
very much to lift, and then he had to let it
drag on the ground, so that it was continually catching in the roots of the grass. It
made him very hot and tired, but he perse-
vered, he could not think of returning to
his small rake after what Jerry had said.
His words had been few, but they had
spoiled Cosmo's pleasure for the day. When
his grandfather came back he was still tug-
ging at the rake.

"What! my boy," said he, "have you
broken your own rake so soon, that you wish
to use mine?"

"No, sir," said Cosmo, without looking up,
"but I thought I would try this."

"Ah! I see how it is," said Mr. Linton,
smiling, "you think it is more manly to use
the large one; but I will tell you something
to remember: never try to seem what you

are not; and it is better to be Cosmo Linton, able to do well whatever you undertake, than to be striving always to do what is beyond your strength. Why, it is just as if my young steers should try to draw a heavy load of hay, instead of the oxen; but come," he continued, "let us go and see Whitefoot— didn't you tell me that you would like to have her near the house? I have a strong cord in my pocket with which to lead her, and we can take her now. I am getting to be too old a man to work all day in the hot sun."

Cosmo gladly shouldered his rake, and followed his grandfather, not forgetting to gather a few clover-heads which, growing in the corner of the field close by some black-berry bushes, had escaped the mower's scythe.

"So much for being in an obscure place," said Mr. Linton, as Cosmo picked them, "they have escaped being cut down by being out of the way."

"But maybe they would as lief be cut down, as to be eaten by my calf," replied Cosmo, now quite cheerful again.

Whitefoot was drinking by the brook, and Cosmo called her, holding out the clover as he did so. She raised her head and tried to reach the clover from the other side of the brook, but she could not; then she put one foot into the brook, and then the other, until she was standing entirely in the water. Cosmo, standing on the edge of the brook, fed her with clover, while his grandfather dexterously slipped the noose, which he had made in the end of the rope, over her head, and then giving it to Cosmo he led her home.

There was an orchard just back of the house where Mr. Linton told Cosmo to take Whitefoot. He tied her to one of the trees while he went into the house to get some salt for her. She licked it from his hand very readily, and then he untied the rope and let her run about the field. His grandfather told him that he must not forget to take her water every day, so that she would not miss the brook which was in her last pasture.

When Cosmo went into the house he found that his grandmother had a letter from his father. They were all well at home, and missed their little boy sadly. He wanted Cosmo to write him a letter every week. Cosmo was glad to hear from home, but he did not like the idea of writing letters very much.

"You see, grandmamma," said he, "I have no time for writing letters; now that it is haying-time, grandpapa wants me to help him."

"Oh! I guess he'll excuse you long enough to write to your mother," said Mrs. Linton, smiling, "you know a letter from you will make her just as happy as this letter has made you." Cosmo shook his head, but he made no reply; the truth was, he loved to work in the hay-field much better than to write letters.

At dinner his grandmother asked when the hay was to be brought in.

"Why," said Mr. Linton, "I had intended to leave it until to-morrow, but the sun has been so hot that it is pretty well dried, and as it may rain to-morrow, I think I will draw it in this afternoon."

"O grandpapa!" said Cosmo, "may I ride on the hay-cart?"

"To be sure you may, only don't get smothered in the hay."

"Oh! no fear of that!" replied Cosmo, as he hastened to finish his dinner, that he might be all ready to ride to the field.

The pudding had just come on to the table smoking hot, when Cosmo heard one of the men driving the oxen down the lane which led from the barn. "O grandmamma! may I go," he exclaimed, "I don't want any pudding." He scarcely waited to hear her answer, when he seized his hat and was bounding down the lane after the hay-cart.

"The dear boy!" said Mrs. Linton, as she looked affectionately after him, "how he does enjoy being here."

"Yes," said his grandfather, "and he is so anxious to be able to do every thing just as grown-up people do. Yesterday I found him trying to harness one of the horses, and to-day he tried to use my rake instead of the small one which I bought for him."

"Just like poor Luther; and I think he looks like him too," said Mrs. Linton, with a sigh.

"I have thought so a great many times," was the reply; and the old gentleman took off his spectacles and wiped them before he could read his son's letter, which he held in his hand.

What the remembrance was, which so saddened Cosmo's grandparents, I will tell my young readers in another chapter.

CHAPTER V.

Cosmo had a grand time that afternoon, riding on the hay. He got on the cart after the men had thrown a little hay on it, and then as they threw more he packed it and pressed it down. Sometimes Caleb would throw a great bundle of hay right over him, and it would be a minute or two before he could extricate himself, and then when the load was ready to take to the barn, and he rode on the top of it, he thought it was the nicest ride he had ever had, except once when he had been to the menagerie, and rode on an elephant; he thought riding on the hay was something like that, for he seemed just as high in the air, and he swung back and forth in the same manner. He was thinking of this when they reached the barn.

"Take care, heads down!" said Caleb, who was driving the oxen, and Cosmo had just time enough to lie flat down on the hay, when the oxen went right into the barn. The hay was piled up so high that there was just room enough for it to go in the door, and so Cosmo's head would not have been very safe if Caleb had not warned him. Then came the unloading. Cosmo jumped on to the mow and helped to spread it out evenly. He was not the only one who enjoyed it: it was a grand feasting-time to the chickens and ducks. They flocked round the cart, and as the grasshoppers hopped off from the hay, wondering at this disturbance of their homes, they swallowed them so fast that the poor things had not time to wonder very long.

The afternoon passed away very happily to Cosmo, and before the sun was down, all the hay was safe in the barn, and he told his grandmother at the tea-table, as he ate the pudding which she had saved for him, that he thought bringing in the hay was the greatest fun of all.

But I must not forget to tell you of one adventure which Cosmo had that afternoon, and which gave him a great deal of trouble for a little while. When he rode back to the field with Caleb the second time, the men were not quite ready to begin to load yet, so he went to the fence to see if he could find some blackberries on the bushes. He found a few which he ate, and was just going back to Caleb, when he saw some very fine ones on a branch almost hidden behind the rest.

"I must have those at any rate," he said, as he pulled aside the bushes with one hand, and thrust the other into the opening thus made. But in an instant he drew it back with a loud scream. "Oh! it's a snake! it's a snake! I know it is," he screamed, as one of the men came towards him, "and it has bitten my hand!"

His grandfather came into the field just

then. "Oh! no," said he, as he looked at
Cosmo's hand, "that is a hornet's sting, you
must have disturbed a nest some where."
And sure enough there in the bushes, close
to Cosmo's fine blackberries, was a hornets'
nest, and one of the hornets, not liking his
intrusion, had stung his hand.

"Ha! ha!" said Mr. Linton, "this nest
must be destroyed; don't forget, Caleb, to
burn it up some evening."

"Very well, sir," said Caleb, as he went
back to his work.

The pain was pretty severe for a little
while, but Cosmo would not go the house
What would Jerry say, if he should care so
much for a hornet's sting—he might call him
a baby with truth. No, no! he was going
to see all the hay in before he went home.
So he mounted the cart again and tried to
forget the pain. When he did go home
the pain was all gone, but his hand was
very much swollen. His grandmother applied something to it which she said would

make it well; and sure enough, the next morning the swelling was all gone, and there was nothing left to remind him of Mr. Hornet but a little red spot where his sting had pierced the skin.

A shower came on that evening, so that Caleb could not burn the hornets' nest as he intended. Days passed by, and Cosmo had forgotten all about it, when one evening at the tea-table, his grandfather told him that Caleb was going to burn up the hornets' nest that evening, and he might go and see him do it.

Of course, Cosmo was glad to go; and when Caleb came for some alcohol, which Mrs. Linton gave him in a tin cup, Cosmo was all ready for a start.

"But what are you going to do with alcohol?" asked Cosmo, as they walked along.

"Oh! you'll see," was the reply, for Caleb did not like to have questions asked him.

It was not quite dark when they reached the field, but the hornets were all in their nest. That was the reason that Caleb waited for the evening that he might be sure to kill them all. Cosmo noticed that Caleb carried a long pole, and when they reached the place where the nest was, he took some pieces of cotton cloth from his pocket and tied them on to the end of it with a piece of cord.

"Now for the alcohol," said Caleb, "and you'll see what I am going to do with it."

Cosmo held the cup, and Caleb dipped the end of the pole in it, until the cloth was soaked with alcohol. Then he gave it to Cosmo to hold, while he took some matches from his pocket, and lighting one, he set fire to the cloth which burnt at once with a blue flame.

"Now stand back," said he.

Cosmo moved back, and Caleb, holding one end of the pole applied the lighted end to the nest, and in a moment it was all in a blaze. A few hornets flew out, but Caleb knocked them down, and soon they were all destroyed.

Cosmo became quite excited, and ran up and down the field screaming, " Fire ! Fire !" just as he had heard men cry in the city

But the fire did not last very long, for the nest soon burned up, and the bushes were too green to take fire.   There was no danger of setting fire to the fence, for that was of stone.

The next day after the fire, happened to be rainy, so as Cosmo could not go out, his grandmother proposed that he should write to his mother.

He consented very willingly, for he was in want of some amusement. So he went up to his room, and took his new portfolio which his mother had given him out of his trunk, and laid it on the desk which his father had used when he was a boy.

The portfolio was well stocked with paper and pens, but he had no ink; so his grandmother lent him her inkstand.

Cosmo could write pretty well in his copy-book at school, but he was not much accustomed to letter-writing, so it took him a good while to fill two pages.

After he had finished his letter, he took it to his grandmother to read.

I think he would let you read it too. It was as follows:

MY DEAR MOTHER: I like to be here very much, though I want to see you too. Grandpa lets me help him make hay. I like taking it into the barn best.

One day I went to the mill with grandpa. I saw the corn ground. I met a boy there, and his name is James Ford. He is the miller's son. He asked me to come to see him, and grandpapa says I may go.

Last night there was a fire near here, and a house was burned down. All the family were burned up too, for they were asleep. I saw it, and called out, "Fire!" but no one came to put it out.

It rains to-day, and that is the reason I am writing to you. I wish you would come here, and papa too. Give my love to him, and to grandmamma and Margaret.

Your affectionate son,

COSMO P. LINTON.

His grandmother smiled as she read the account of the fire, but she said: "I think your mamma will be alarmed when she reads about the fire if you don't tell her what it means. You had better add a postscript and tell her whose house it was."

"Well, I will," he replied, "only I am tired of writing."

"It will not take you very long," said Mrs. Linton.

So he added the following

P. S.—Grandmamma says I had better tell you whose house burnt down. It was Mr. and Mrs. Hornet's house, and all the little Hornets were burned. Caleb set it on fire, because one of them stung me.

His grandmother said that would do, and

then she folded the letter for him and put it in an envelope, which she directed, as he thought he could not write well enough for that, and then he put a postage-stamp on it.

In the afternoon the weather cleared, and his grandfather took him to the post-office, where he put his letter in the letter-box.

CHAPTER VI.

Cosmo enjoyed Sunday at his grand. father's very much. At first he thought he should not, for he could not go fishing or berrying, or work with the men in the field, but he found there were pleasures for the Sabbath as well as the other days. He liked the singing of the birds, which awakened him every Sunday morning; he thought they sang louder and more sweetly than on any other day, and perhaps they did, although Cosmo's grandmamma suggested that perhaps it seemed so because there were no other sounds to break the stillness of the morning. At any rate, Cosmo loved to hear them very much, particularly the robin which had built its nest on the limb of the cherry tree close to his window. It was so close that he could almost look inside of the nest. And every

Sunday morning the robin warbled so sweetly, seeming to say, "Wake up and enjoy with me this lovely Sabbath morning."

Then Cosmo would get up and dress himself carefully for church. After he was dressed, he would read his chapter, which when he was at home, he always read with his mother, and then offer his morning prayer.

After breakfast and prayers, he would select some of the interesting Sunday books which his father had sent for him, and which his grandmother only gave him on Sunday, and go to the seat under the large elm near the house, and read until church time.

He liked sitting there very much, because it was close to the garden, and the breeze as it blew towards him came scented with the perfume of the pinks and other sweet flowers which grew there; and he liked to hear the soft hum of the insects, as they too seemed to be singing their Sabbath hymn of praise. At nine o'clock they started for church, for they had to ride four miles, and as the service began at ten, his grandfather started so as to be there a little before the time. He said: " He did not like to hurry into church and get there only just in time to commence with the minister; he liked to have a few moments to consider into whose presence he was approaching, that he might do so with reverence."

So always at nine o'clock the farm-wagon came to the door with Jerry for driver. Cosmo's grandfather went to church in the wagon instead of the carriage, because it would hold them all, and he liked to give all in his house the privilege of going to church. Cosmo always jumped in immediately, and took his place by Jerry, then his grandfather helped his grandmother in. She always sat on the middle seat. And after Abby and Sophy had seated themselves on the back-seat, his grandfather locked the front-door, and putting the key in his pocket took his place on the middle seat, when they drove off.

This drive was always a very pleasant one to Cosmo. They met a great many wagons all carrying families to church; and the fields as they passed them seemed sleeping in the Sabbath stillness, resting from the reaper and the hay-maker.

When they reached the church door they always found a number of people standing around outside.

Cosmo's grandparents and the servants went directly into the church, but Cosmo remained in the wagon with Jerry and drove with him around the back of the church where there was a long shed, under which were several horses and wagons. Jerry drove under it and fastened the horses, and then Jerry and Cosmo went to the church. Jerry generally remained standing by the door, until the service commenced, and Cosmo would have liked sometimes to stay there with him, but his grandfather preferred that he should always come directly to his seat, so he always did.

The first Sunday that Cosmo went to church in this way, he had noticed with some surprise, that his grandmother when she got into the wagon had a large black merino bag, which she carried very carefully, and that Abby and Sophy had one too. They seemed to be full of something, and he wondered what that something was. But he forgot to ask about them after they started, though he meant to do so, he was so much taken up with the pleasure of driving to church. But after the service was over in the morning he found out what the bags contained, and as you may have wondered as much as he did, I will tell you.

The afternoon service commenced at one o'clock, and as the intermission was so short, scarcely any one went home until afterwards, for most of the people lived at a distance from church. So they waited in the church or around the door until one o'clock came. Cosmo's grandmother remained in her pew when the people went out, but Cosmo rushed out with the rest; at the door he saw Abby and Sophy just opening their bags. They took from them a biscuit and gingerbread, which they had brought for their luncheon.

"O Cosmo!" said Sophy, as soon as she saw him, "your grandmamma has some luncheon for you in her bag; you had better go and ask her for it."

"So, ho!" said Cosmo to himself, as he went back, "that was what the bags had in them, was it?" He met his grandmother coming out, bag in hand. He followed her to an elm tree at one side of the church, where she sat down on a bench which was there, and opened the mysterious bag. Cosmo found the biscuits and gingerbread which it contained very good. After he had eaten it, she gave him a little pewter cup, which she also carried in her bag, and told him that he could go and find Jerry, and he would tell him where to get some water for her. Jerry was standing at the door, and he went with Cosmo very readily. He seemed

very good-natured; indeed, he had not tried
to tease Cosmo once that day, and Cosmo
wondered as he went along whether it was
because it was Sunday. Jerry took him to a
house quite near the church, which had a well
close by it, and then Jerry drew some water,
and filling the cup gave it to Cosmo, while
he took a drink from the bucket. Cosmo
would have liked to drink from the bucket
too, but he was afraid to do so, lest he might
spill some water on his clothes, and then
Jerry would laugh at him. So he contented
himself with drinking from the cup as Jerry
told him to do, and then refilling it took it to
his grandmother. She asked him if he
would like to go into the churchyard with
her. The Sunday-school which was always
held in the intermission, in the galleries of
the church, had commenced, but as Cosmo
was only to be there three or four Sundays,
his grandmother had not thought it best for
him to attend.

Cosmo was very ready to go with his

grandmamma, for he thought she might tell him some interesting story, as she often did. So he ran before her to the neat iron gate, and opening it, he held it open for her to pass in. Then he shut the gate softly, and walked slowly by her side; for all around him the dead were sleeping, and it seemed so quiet and peaceful there, that he did not feel like running and jumping as he had before. His grandmamma seemed to be occupied with her own thoughts, and said nothing to him until they reached an inclosure in one corner of the graveyard, which was surrounded by a fence, neatly painted white. There were several grave-stones in it, and in the centre a willow-tree was growing, the branches of which spread so widely, that they nearly touched all the graves. Under the tree was a rustic seat. Cosmo's grandmother opened the gate to this inclosure, and went in, and Cosmo followed. She seated herself under the tree, as if she felt quite as much at home there as

in her own parlor, motioning to Cosmo to
take a seat beside her.   He did so, and as for
a few minutes his grandmamma. said nothing,
he looked at the inscriptions upon the stones.
On two of them were the names of his
father's grandparents, and then he knew that
this inclosure was his grandfather's family
burial - place.   On the opposite side from
these, were three little graves, two very
short; with the inscription: "Infant children
of George and Mary Linton."   The date of
their death was many years before Cosmo
was born.   They were the graves of his father's
two sisters, who had died in infancy.   The
third grave was much longer than these, but
was evidently one of a child.   Cosmo read:
"In memory of Luther Linton, who died
August 5th."   "Why, grandmamma," he exclaimed, " it is the same day of the month as
this, just my age too—nine years.   Was he
my father's brother?"

"Yes, Cosmo," said his grandmamma;
"and it was just thirty years ago to-day,

that he went out as well and strong as you are, and was brought home to me dead."

"O grandmamma! how dreadful. Won't you tell me how it all happened? I have never heard my father speak of him."

"He was too young when Luther died, to remember any thing about him; but I brought you here to-day to tell you his story. This willow-tree your grandfather planted a little sapling the autumn after he was buried here, and see what a great tree it is. A few years ago, he had this seat made here for me, because I have always liked every pleasant Sunday to spend part of the noon intermission here. And I love to sit here, and think of the many years my son has been with his Saviour, and of the day when his body, now mingled with the dust, will rise again. Not many years and I shall be sleeping by his side, and together we shall hear the archangel trumpet, and rise to glory. For though Luther was taken away so suddenly, he was not unprepared to die.

8*

One evening, some months before his death, he came to me in tears, telling me that he had been thinking what a sinner he was, and asked me if I thought Jesus would forgive him. I told him that the blood of Jesus cleanses from all sin, and as we were alone in my room, I proposed that we should kneel down together, and pray for forgiveness. We did so, and he was such a child, that his expressions of sorrow for sin, and desires to be made a child of God, astonished me. I was sure that he had been taught by the Spirit. After I had prayed with him, and we arose from our knees, he clasped his arms around my neck and begged me to forgive all his disobedience to me, and said he meant from this time to be a child of God, and to try to keep His commandments.

"From that night I saw a great change in him; he was so much more gentle than he used to be, and more yielding to my wishes. He was very constant in secret prayer, also. I do not think he ever left his room in the morning or went to bed at night, without reading God's word, and offering a prayer. He was a very daring boy, never seeming to think of danger, and like you, Cosmo, he wanted to do every thing which a man could do. He wanted to be a help to his father on the farm; and he was always anxious to do the hardest work. I was often afraid he would get hurt, but he promised me to be careful, and his father thought I was too fearful. But when I saw him climbing trees, and riding the horses, which were none of the gentlest, I was always anxious. One day, just after dinner, your grandfather wanted to drive to the village, so he sent the boy who lived with us then, to harness the horses for him. They had not been used for two or three days, and had been in the pasture-lot, feeding. They were young horses, and quite spirited, and they had enjoyed their liberty so long that they did not care to be caught. So when the boy went to catch them he had a great deal of

difficulty. They would come up to eat the
salt which he offered them, but just as he
went to lay his hand on them, off they would
gallop. He was just going to call one of the
men when Luther came along; he saw what
trouble Zeke, as we always called him, was in,
and calling out that he would help him, he
sprang over the fence. 'Now, Zeke,' said
he, 'you hold the salt, and I will come and
throw the halter over Hero's neck.' Zeke
wanted Luther to hold the salt, and he
would throw the bridle, but Luther would
not consent. As I said before, he always
chose to do what seemed the hardest. Hero
came very willingly to eat the salt, but as
he saw Luther approaching with the halter,
he guessed his intention, and throwing up his
heels away he galloped. Luther was not
prepared for this, and he was standing so
near the horse that as Hero threw up his
hind-legs, his iron shoe struck the boy's forehead, and he fell to the ground. Zeke went
to him and lifted him up, but he just groaned

once, and never breathed again. Some men
who were passing, helped Zeke carry our
poor boy to the house. Your grandfather
who had become impatient at the delay, and
had gone out to see why Zeke did not come,
met them at the gate. He came back to
prepare me for it, but the sight of his face
was enough. I knew something dreadful
had happened, and in a few moments I knew
all. Every means to restore him was tried,
but in vain ; he had died almost the instant
the horse had struck him. Oh ! I thought
if I had only tried to induce him to be more
careful. My only consolation was, that he
had gone to be with Jesus."

Cosmo had listened with great attention to
his grandmamma's story. He felt that he was
like Luther in wishing to do every thing which
men could do, and in trying to seem older than
he was ; but ah ! was he like him in loving
the Saviour and trying to please Him? He
could not say " Yes," in his heart to that, and

as he read the words on Luther's tombstone,
" Be ye also ready, for at such an hour as ye
think not, the Son of Man cometh," the words
seemed to be spoken to him.   The bell was
ringing for church, when his grandmamma
had finished her story, so she had no more
time to talk with him.   She stooped to pick
a flower from Luther's grave as she left the
inclosure, and Cosmo followed her example.
He tried to be very attentive in church that
afternoon, and as they rode home, he did not
feel as much like talking to Jerry as he had
in the morning.

The Sabbath was the happiest day in the
week to Mrs. Linton, and she tried to make
it a happy day for every one in her house.
Cosmo thought it was the pleasantest of all
the week.   He told his mother when he went
home, that his grandmamma always had a
better dinner on Sunday than any other day.
His mother wondered at that, for she knew
that they all went to church ; but the truth

was this, Cosmo's grandmother always prepared her Sunday dinner on Saturday; and
this, all the while that Cosmo was there, was
a chicken-pie, baked on Saturday, and put in
the oven and heated after they came home
from church. Now Cosmo loved chicken-pie
better than any thing, so he always had
pleasant associations connected with the
Sunday dinner at his grandfather's.

There was an old-fashioned Bible full of
pictures, in his grandmother's parlor, which
Cosmo always looked at every Sunday afternoon. It rested on a small table near one of
the windows, and he used to draw his chair
up by it, while his grandfather sat reading in
his easy-chair by the other window. The
ticking of the old clock standing in the
corner, was a pleasant sound to him, and the
jars on the high old-fashioned mantel-piece,
which were always filled with fresh flowers
on Saturday, and the bright green asparagus
branches in the fire-place, gave the room a
very cheerful look.

Sometimes his grandfather would lay aside his book and explain the pictures to Cosmo, and tell him some of the stories from the Bible. There was also an old *Pilgrim's Progress* full of pictures, which Cosmo was never tired of looking at. There was one picture of Christian in Doubting Castle, which always made Cosmo out of patience. "To think," he used to say "that Christian who had conquered in so many battles, should not try to kill that old Giant Despair, and fight his way out of that castle."

"But you must remember," his grandpapa would say, "that it was only by the help of the key called Promise, that they could get out. Ah! my boy, when the Christian, by yielding to sin, is seized by Giant Despair, he only can get peace of mind by remembering the promises of God to pardon sin, and by calling upon Him for forgiveness.

Sometimes just at sunset both of Cosmo's grandparents would walk with him by the side of the brook, or in the garden, and talk together so sweetly of the love of God, in making all the beautiful things which surrounded them, that Cosmo would feel his heart swell, and he would long to love Him too as they did.

CHAPTER VII.

Two weeks passed very happily for Cosmo at his grandfather's, very much in the same manner that the first few days had passed. He had not become tired of his pet calf, but he had been so constant in feeding her, that she had learned to know him quite well, and would run towards him whenever she saw him come into the orchard, and rub her head against him, and lick his hand, as if she knew that he was her friend.

But after awhile, Cosmo began to be a little tired of playing alone. He missed the boys who were his playmates at home. And one day, after spending the morning in fishing without catching many fish, he went home to dinner, determined to ask his grandfather if he could not go and invite James Ford to come and play with him that very afternoon. Just as he was coming up the lane, however, by the side of the house, intending to leave his fish in the kitchen, he saw the stage which brought passengers from the steamboat, drive up to the front-gate. A gentleman jumped out of it, and then lifted out a little girl, who was not so large as Cosmo. The driver took from the top of the stage a small trunk, which he left on the front-piazza, and then the stage drove off, and the travellers entered the house.

Cosmo hurried into the kitchen to ask Abby and Sophy who they were. But they could not give him any information; so leaving his fish, he went up the back-stairs to his own room without going in to see the new-comers. This he did partly because he knew that his mother would not like him to be seen without first washing his face and hands and brushing his hair, and partly because he felt a little shy about seeing strangers. While he was in his room, he heard them come up-stairs with his grandmother. The gentleman went into the room on the opposite side of the hall, called the north chamber. It was the room always occupied by visitors. The little girl his grandmamma brought into her room, and then into a small room which was between her room and the north chamber. Cosmo heard his grandmother say: "I will give you this room, Ettie, so that you will be close by me. Your cousin Cosmo has a room on the other side of me, so you see I shall have both my children near me."

"Oh!" said Cosmo to himself, "now I know who they are. They are my Uncle Selby and my Cousin Ettie. I wonder if she has come to stay long, and if she knows how to play," and he felt quite pleased at the thought of having a playmate.

Ettie, as Cosmo's grandmamma called her, though her real name was Viletta, was the daughter of the only sister of Cosmo's father, who lived in the western part of the country, and seldom came to visit her friends. Cosmo had never seen her or any of his cousins, though Mr. Selby, who came to New-York every year on business, had told him all about them, and had promised to bring Ettie with him some time. He had now fulfilled his promise, and Ettie was come to visit her grandparents while he attended to his business in New-York.

As soon as Cosmo had made himself look neatly, he went down the back-stairs again, and through a narrow passage into the dining-room. No one was there when he entered, but in a few minutes his grandmother appeared, leading his cousin Ettie by the hand. She was a gentle-looking little girl, with light curling hair, and when she laid her hand timidly in Cosmo's, and put up her mouth for a kiss, when her grandmamma introduced them, Cosmo thought she was very pretty. He did not say so, however, and a stranger would have thought that he was not glad to see her at all. For as soon as he had kissed her he turned round and looked out of the window as if there was some curiosity on the lawn which he must examine. But you and I, who know boys and girls so well, know that they were both very glad to see each other, only they felt very shy, and did not know what to say first, so they said nothing.

Cosmo did not have to look out of the window very long, for in a minute his grandfather came in, delighted to see his little granddaughter; then Mr. Selby came downstairs, and they sat down to dinner.

"You see, Cosmo," said Ettie's father, "I was as good as my word, only you were not at home when I brought Ettie, so I had to bring her out here to see you."

"And very glad we are to see her," said his grandmother; "it carries me back to the days when their father and mother were children, to see them together."

"You'll have a great deal to show Ettie after dinner, Cosmo," said his grandfather; "there's your calf, and the chickens, and the brook."

"Yes," said Cosmo, "and the horses, and the hay which we have brought in."

His grandfather smiled, as he thought that Ettie would not care much for those, but he did not say so, for he knew that Cosmo would feel embarrassed, and think they were laughing at him if he did.

Mr. Selby was obliged to return to New-York the next morning; so immediately after dinner Cosmo's grandfather took him out in the wagon to see the country, while the children were left to amuse themselves. And first Cosmo took Ettie out to the orchard to see his calf. By the time they reached it all their shyness was gone, and they were chatting as merrily as if they had known each other always.

"Oh! what a little beauty!" exclaimed Ettie, as soon as she saw Whitefoot; "and how tame she is!" she continued, as she saw her lick the salt from Cosmo's hand. "I wonder if she will eat from mine," and she held out her little hand to the calf. Whitefoot did not come to Ettie quite so readily as she did to Cosmo, but after looking at her a few moments, I rather think she liked the looks of her curls as well as Cosmo did, for she came up to her and began to lick her hand, just as she had done his. Ettie did not quite like the feeling of her rough tongue, and she drew back her hand rather quickly, before poor Whitefoot had time to eat all the salt.

"What is her name?" said Ettie.

"Whitefoot."

"Oh! I would have called her Lily, she is so white."

"Poh! that is a girl's name," said Cosmo contemptuously. "I think Whitefoot is a great deal better name for a calf, and besides her mother's name is Whitey."

"Oh! that makes a difference," said Ettie gently, for she saw that Cosmo was a little vexed, and she had not meant to vex him.

"Come," said Cosmo, "let's go to the barn and find some eggs." There was a ladder resting against the hay-mow, and the children climbed by means of it upon the hay. In one corner the hens had made a nest, and there were six eggs in it. Cosmo took five of them out carefully, and put them into his hat. But he left one in the nest, because his grandmamma had told him to do so. She said that the hens would not lay a second time in a place from which all the eggs had been taken. After Cosmo had put his hat with the eggs in it in one corner of the hay-mow, where they were in no danger of being broken, he said: "Now, Ettie, let's play hide and seek in the hay."

"Well," said Ettie, "you hide first."

So she sat down and shut her eyes very tight. In a moment she heard a faint "coop," which sounded as if the person who said it was half-smothered. She opened her eyes, but she could see nothing of Cosmo, and the hay looked as if it had been undisturbed. She listened, but she could hear no sound, but the buzzing of a fly which had been caught in a spider's web in the rafters over her head, and was vainly trying to get out. For a moment she was inclined to feel afraid, it was so still and lonely there. But then she reflected that Cosmo could not be very far off. So she began to search diligently among the hay; she looked in every corner, talking all the time very loudly to Cosmo, to keep up her courage, though she did not know where he was. At last she hit her foot against something hard in the hay, and down she fell. She was up again in a moment though, and pulling away the hay from the place where she fell, what did she find but Cosmo's foot! In a second more she had his head uncovered, and he jumped up.

"There, didn't I cover myself up nicely?" said Cosmo, "why, you walked right over me two or three times without knowing it; and now it is your turn." So saying, he threw himself down full length on the hay with his face resting on his hands, to wait

for Ettie to hide. She tried and tried, but
she could not cover herself with hay, so she
went to Cosmo, and said :

"Won't you come and cover me up? for
as fast as I put the hay on one side, the
other gets uncovered."

Cosmo burst into a loud laugh : "Why,
you silly child, if I should cover you up I
should know where to find you!"

Ettie's face grew very red, and she was
almost ready to cry, for she did not like to
be laughed at; but Cosmo did not mean to
make her feel badly, so he said:

"Never mind, I will show you how, and
then you can hide where you please. See
here, first you make a hollow place in the
hay, like this, and then lie down, and it is
very easy to cover yourself up with the hay
which you have piled up on one side—it will
almost fall over you of itself."

Ettie had quite recovered her good humor
by this time, so she said, "Oh! I see now,"
and went away to try to hide once more.

She had made the hollow place as Cosmo had told her, and was just going to lie down, when she heard a faint "mew." She listened, and she heard it again. She turned in the direction from which the sound proceeded, and there, just behind her, close to the side of the barn, were four little kittens.

"O Cosmo, Cosmo!" she exclaimed, "come here quick, and see what I have found!"

Cosmo was there in an instant. "Poh!" said he, as he looked at them, "nothing but little kittens. I thought you had found a dozen eggs at least."

"I think that kittens are a great deal prettier than eggs," said Ettie, disappointed that her cousin was not as much pleased at her discovery as she was. "They must be very young, for they can hardly stand up; and see, their eyes are tight shut. I think this little white one is the prettiest, don't you?" and Ettie took it in her lap, and stroked it caressingly.

"No," said Cosmo, becoming more interested in the kittens, " I like the gray one the best."

Just then old puss, who had been away to get something to eat, climbed up the post, and came softly towards them. She looked a little suspiciously at Cosmo and Ettie, as if she were afraid they were going to take away her children. She purred over the three little ones who were in her nest, but she did not lie quietly down by them ; she evidently missed the one which was gone. While she was looking for it, she heard it mew, and spying it in Ettie's lap, she sprang up and taking it by the back of the neck, dragged it back to its place, purring over it in a most satisfied manner.

" Oh ! what a cruel cat," exclaimed Ettie, " to carry her kitten so !"

" Oh ! no," said Cosmo, " she is not cruel ; that is the way cats always carry their kittens. But come, don't spend all your time in looking at the kittens: let's play some more. Let us try to cover each other up with hay."

"Well!" said Ettie, and she caught up a great bundle of hay and threw it on him. He scrambled out of it as quickly as he could, and threw hay on her. Ettie was almost covered before she could extricate herself, but she managed to, and then she threw some more hay on him. The children became very much excited in this play, and laughed and screamed so loudly that they did not hear any one come into the barn; so they were quite startled when they heard a gruff voice quite near them exclaiming: "Hallo! there, you youngsters, what are you about, spoiling the hay? Come down, both of you." They stopped their play and turned at the sound, and there, just above the top of the ladder, was Caleb's head with the straw hat, which he always wore, on the top of it.

"We are not spoiling the hay, Caleb," said Cosmo, "we are only playing here."

"Playing or not playing, you must come down," said Caleb; "how do I know but the barn will burn down to-night, in consequence of your mischief? Besides, I had spread the hay all even, so that the new hay which we are going to get in to-morrow might be put on top of it, and now you have got it all in heaps."

Ettie heard with dismay that more hay was to be put there to-morrow. "What will become of the kittens?" she thought; but Caleb seemed so cross that she was afraid to say any thing to him about them. "Come, let us go down," she whispered softly to Cosmo.

"I won't go down," said Cosmo, "this is my grandfather's barn, and I shall stay here, and Caleb has no right to tell me to come down," and he threw himself determinedly down on the hay.

"Very well, I'll see what your grandfather will say," said Caleb, as he disappeared down the ladder. Just then the children heard the sound of wheels, and in a moment more, their grandpapa's voice talking with Caleb. Cosmo lay quite still, while Ettie stood by his side twisting a piece of hay over her finger. They were feeling very uncomfortably when they heard their grandpapa calling out pleasantly:

"Come here, little folks, where have you hid yourselves?"

"Here we are, grandpapa," said Ettie, going to the top of the ladder, "on the hay."

"Why, how did you get there? Can such a little lady as you are climb a ladder?"

"Oh! yes, grandpapa, and see how nicely I can come down!" and Ettie clambered down like a little squirrel, but her grandpapa caught her in his arms, before she got to the bottom.

Cosmo came down more slowly, for he had his hat full of eggs to carry. He was very silent, for he felt conscious that he had not spoken just as he ought to Caleb, though his grandfather treated him just as if nothing had happened, when he was sure that Caleb must have told him all about it. The truth was, his grandfather wanted him to get all over his angry feelings before he spoke to him on the subject. So he said: "Come, Cosmo, show your cousin the way to the pear tree back of the barn; perhaps we can find some ripe pears on it. You can go to the house with your eggs first, if you like." Cosmo went to give his eggs to Abby, and then ran back just as his grandfather and cousin reached the fence which separated the barn-yard from the orchard where the pear tree was.

"Where is papa?" said Ettie.

"Oh! I left him to have a quiet talk with your grandmamma, when I drove to the barn," said her grandfather, as he lifted the little girl over the fence. The pear tree was close by, and as he shook it quite a shower of pears fell off. The children picked them up in a few minutes.

"Let us sit down here and eat one," said

their grandfather, pointing to a log which was near the tree. The children did not wait for a second invitation, but were soon enjoying one of the mellow juicy pears.

"What is this, Cosmo?" said his grandfather, "that Caleb tells me about your playing in the hay?"

"Why, grandpapa, we were having such fine fun in the hay-mow, and Caleb came and ordered us down, and I told him that I wouldn't come, for I didn't think he had any right to tell me to come down."

"What do you think I hire Caleb for?" said his grandfather.

"Why, to work on the farm, I suppose."

"Yes, and to take care of my property. Don't you think if he saw some boys helping themselves to these pears, he would have a right to drive them away?"

"Oh! yes, but then I am your grandson, and have as much right in the barn as he has."

"Well, then, if one of my cows got in the

corn-field, would not Caleb do right to drive her out?"

"But she would do mischief, and I was not doing any harm.

"Who do you think is the best judge of that, a little boy, or a man who has been accustomed to make hay all his life?"

"Why, the man, I suppose," said Cosmo, looking a little ashamed. "But you never told me not to play in the hay."

"No, because I never thought of your doing so."

"But, grandpapa," said Ettie; "what did Caleb mean by saying that the barn might burn down? How could our playing in the hay set it on fire?"

"Some people think that when hay is brought in before it is quite dry, jumping on it and packing it very closely will cause it to take fire. Very likely Caleb thinks so. I do not believe that is true, but Caleb's other reason that the hay was all spread evenly for another load, is enough. You see, Cosmo, he was only taking care of my property, as it is his duty to do when he told you to come down, and I am very sorry that you answered him as you did."

"I am sorry too," said Cosmo.

"I wish you would tell him so, it would please me very much," said his grandpapa.

Cosmo sat still for a moment and then rose and walked towards the barn where he knew Caleb was feeding the horses.

"Caleb," said he; "I am sorry that I answered you so, this afternoon; I did not know that we could do any harm to the hay."

"Well, well, lad," said Caleb as he took Cosmo's offered hand; "we'll say no more about it. May be I was too rough in telling you to come down, but you see I did not like the hay to be spoiled."

While Cosmo had gone to speak to Caleb, Ettie told her grandfather about the kittens, and how she was afraid that they would be smothered if another load of hay was piled on top of them.

"To be sure they will," said her grandfather; "and I will tell Jerry to get them down this evening, and put them in a box in the corner of the barn, where you can go to see them whenever you like."

"Well, my boy," he continued, as Cosmo approached.   "Is it all right?"

"Yes, sir;" said Cosmo, smiling; "it is all right."

"Now I am sure you will not play in the hay again," said his grandfather, as they walked towards the house, "if I tell you I do not wish you too.   But in order to give you some amusement I am going to have a swing and a see-saw put up in the orchard where Whitefoot lives.   There is an old apple tree there which is quite tall, but the apples are not good for much, so I will have some of the lower limbs sawed off, and a swing put up in one of the upper branches. It shall be done to-morrow, and I will send for a carpenter to make you a see-saw."

"Oh! what a good, kind grandpapa you are," said Ettie, and she kissed affectionately the hand which clasped hers. Cosmo danced a regular hornpipe in his excess of joy.

Tea was all ready when they entered the house, and after they left the table, Cosmo and Ettie had so much to tell about their play in the afternoon, and the swing and the see-saw, and they both talked together, and talked so fast, that Ettie's father put up both his hands to his ears in dismay: "One at a time, if you please; what is this, Ettie, the kittens are going to have a swing, and there is going to be an apple tree and a see-saw up in the hay-mow?"

"No, no," said Ettie, laughing so that she nearly fell off from his lap, where she had seated herself when she began to talk. "What a funny papa you are!" and she tried to make him understand a little better what she meant.

"I'm sure I don't know what your grandmamma will do if you are always going to talk so fast as this," said her papa when she paused for breath.

"Oh! grandmamma loves to see the children happy," said that lady, smiling. "And she will always tell them if they are too noisy."

"I hope they will try to make you happy," said Ettie's papa; "but there are the stars coming one by one to light you to bed; so good night, and be sure to be up to say good-by to me in the morning."

"O papa! I am so sorry that you are going to-morrow," said Ettie, as she kissed him good night. "How I wish you could stay all the time with me."

The next morning after they had had breakfast, and Ettie's papa had gone, the children and their grandfather went out to the orchard to see the tree where the swing was to be placed. It was a fine, large apple tree, with wide-spreading branches, but there were very few apples upon it, and they were covered with spots of black mould, so that they would never ripen. Cosmo's grandfather had engaged a carpenter to come that day to make a new cow-shed, but he let him put up the swing and see-saw before he commenced his other work. He sawed off several of the lower limbs of the apple tree, and then he tied a strong rope which Cosmo's grandfather had bought the day before, to one of the upper branches. After both ends were fastened he descended the tree, and made a seat for the swing out of a piece of board which he had, cutting little notches out of each end, for the rope to fit in. When it was all completed, both the children declared that they had never seen a nicer swing, and were both eager to try it. Cosmo being the nearest to it, jumped in first.

"O Cosmo!" said his grandfather, "that is hardly polite. Ettie should swing first."

"Why, I am the oldest, grandpapa."

"Yes, but she is a little girl, and the rule is, girls and ladies first. So jump out, and give Ettie the place."

Cosmo did as his grandfather told him, but with a very bad grace, saying to himself, as Ettie was lifted into the swing: "I don't see why girls are so much better than boys."

Ettie saw that Cosmo was disappointed, so she said: "Don't swing me very long, grandpapa, so that Cosmo can have his turn."

"Hold tight, Ettie," said he, as he began to push her. Up, up, up, she went, until her feet touched the branches of the next apple-tree, and she screamed with delight.

"Are you afraid, Ettie?" said her grandpapa.

"Oh! no, it is so nice," she replied, "I wonder if the birds feel so when they fly through the air."

Her grandfather gave her thirty pushes, and then he "let the cat die." Every child

11

who knows any thing about swinging knows what that means.

When her feet touched the ground, Ettie stopped herself, and gave her place to Cosmo, and his grandfather swung him.

He was as much delighted as Ettie, only he thought it was rather beneath his dignity to make such a fuss about it, so he did not scream as she did.

While the children were swinging, the carpenter was at work on the other side of the tree making a see-saw. And as soon as Cosmo had finished swinging, they went to see him.

He had fastened a wooden thing which carpenters call a horse, and which they use to rest boards on, in the ground; and now he was trying to balance a planed board upon it.

"Make the board a little longer on one side than the other," said their grandfather; "for Ettie is not quite so heavy as Cosmo."

"Now let us see how nicely you can see-saw," he continued, as the carpenter said it was all finished.

"I am glad that we can both try it together," said Ettie, as she took her seat on the end of the board which rested on the ground. Cosmo got on at the middle, and climbed up to the upper end.

There was a long wooden peg at each end of the see-saw for the children to take hold of; so there was no danger of their falling off.

"There is one thing you must remember, children," said their grandfather, before he left them, "to be careful how you get off. I think the best way is for you, Cosmo, when Ettie is on the end nearest the ground, to slip down to the horse which holds the board, and then jump off; then there will be no danger of her being hurt. But if you get off when your end is on the ground, her end will go down suddenly, and she will be knocked off."

Cosmo readily promised, and his grand-

father left them to give directions to the
carpenter about building the cow-shed.

For a while, the children got on very well
together. Cosmo got off several times, but
it must have been only to see how nicely he
could slide down the board, for he got on
again immediately. At last, Ettie thought
she heard Caleb driving the hay-cart to the
barn.

" O Cosmo !" she exclaimed, " let me off.
I want to see if grandpapa remembered to
tell Jerry about the kittens, for there is Caleb
with the hay, and they will be smothered if
they are there."

But Cosmo's end of the see-saw was then
nearest the ground, and he was not willing
to stop see-sawing yet, so he would not let
Ettie down.

" Nonsense !" said Cosmo, " you need not
trouble yourself about the kittens. Of
course grandpapa has told Jerry about them.
I don't want to stop see-sawing yet."

" Please, Cosmo, let me off," pleaded Ettie.

"I do want to go to see the kittens so much."

"You can see them afterwards," said Cosmo, still keeping the little girl in the air. "I have not see-sawed half enough yet," now feeling a little disposition to tease.

"Oh! there, I see Caleb driving in the barn, the kittens will be smothered, I must get off," said Ettie, quite terrified at the thought.

But Cosmo sat quite still and only smiled. Ettie burst into tears. Cosmo felt sorry then, but he would not own it.

"Just like girls," said he, "always crying at every little thing. I don't think much of them to play with any how." And he gave a spring and landed Ettie safe on the ground.

"Now, sit still," said he, "until I get off," and slipping down the board he jumped to the ground, while Ettie ran to the barn to see about the kittens. Cosmo was too much out of humor to follow her, so he went to feed Whitefoot.

"You are the best play-fellow, after all," said he, as the little animal ran to meet him. "You never cry, do you, Whitefoot?" and he laid his cheek caressingly against White-foot's head. Cosmo forgot how hard it had been for him not to cry when Jerry had teased him.

Ettie found Jerry just taking the kittens down, while Caleb stood waiting to put the hay up. But Jerry had forgotten to fix any other place for them, so Ettie held them in her lap, while he got a box and put some hay in for a bed. Old puss was absent while all this was going on, but she came back before the box was quite ready for them, and she seemed quite distressed to see her kittens in Ettie's lap. She walked round and round her, mewing piteously, and seeming to take no notice of Ettie when she told her that she was going to have a nice new home. Perhaps she did not understand her. At last the box was all prepared, and Ettie put the kittens in and puss jumped in after them, settling herself by their side with a motherly mew and purr.

Ettie stood still watching puss part of the time as she caressed her kittens, and gave them a good washing to comfort them for her long absence. And then as she looked at Caleb and Jerry unloading the hay-cart, she wished that Cosmo had not got angry, and that he was there. She was just thinking that she would go back to the orchard, and tell him that she would see-saw again, when Caleb asked her if she would like to ride back to the hay-field.

"Oh! yes, Caleb," was her delighted reply, "may I?"

Caleb made no answer, but lifted her in the hay-cart; then he started the oxen and she went jolting down the lane. She liked it very much, but she wished more than ever for Cosmo.

She found her grandfather in the hay-field, and he seemed very much surprised to see her.

"What, tired of the see-saw so soon?"

said he, as he lifted her out of the cart. "And where is Cosmo?"

"I left him in the orchard," said Ettie. "I went to see the kittens and he did not want to go." This was true, but not all the truth; but she did not want to tell her grandfather that they had had any dispute.

He guessed from her downcast look and faltering tones, that something was wrong, but he did not ask any more questions. He only said: "Would you like to stay here until the cart is loaded, and then you can ride back to the barn on it, and go to the orchard and join Cosmo."

Ettie was very much pleased with this proposal; so she amused herself with trying to toss the hay until Caleb was ready to return to the barn, when she had a nice ride on the load of hay. She liked it better than she did the ride to the field, for the cart did not jolt so much, though she was a little afraid of falling. Just as she reached the barn, she heard the sound of a horn.

"What is that?" she exclaimed.

"I guess it is to call you to dinner," said Caleb. So Ettie ran to the house, and sure enough dinner was all ready.

And while she is eating it, I will tell what Cosmo had been doing all the time that Ettie had been amusing herself with the kittens and in the hay-field. We left him feeding Whitefoot, and making up his mind not to play with girls again. Yet all the time he felt rather uncomfortable, for he was not sure that he had not been the most to blame. After a while, Whitefoot had enough to eat; and he began to look about for some other amusement, when he heard his grand-mamma calling him. Looking up, he saw her standing by the swing; she had come out to see that and the new see-saw. She admired them both very much.

"Why, this is better than the swing you had last summer in the elm-tree, is it not?" said she. "But where is Ettie? I should like to see you both on the see-saw."

Cosmo did not like to tell his grandmamma that they had any disagreement; so he only said: "She went to the barn to see after the kittens."

His grandmamma guessed how matters stood, but she only said: "Let us go and see them too, then." So Cosmo led the way to the barn. When they reached the barn, Jerry who was at work there, said that Ettie had gone with Caleb. The walk was too long to the hay-field through the hot sun for Mrs. Linton. So after admiring the kittens, she turned her steps to the house, saying that she must see the children on the see-saw some other time.

She asked Cosmo if he would not pick some corn to cook for dinner. He willingly consented, and as they walked towards the house for a basket, she said: "It seems to me Cosmo, that you and Ettie have very soon got tired of playing together. Don't you like her for a play-mate?"

"Why, you see, grandmamma, she's a girl, and she cries so easy."

"But did you do any thing to make her cry?"

"No; nothing that she needed to cry for; only she wanted to go after the kittens, and I wanted to see-saw longer; so I kept my end of the board down and hers up for a few minutes, and then she cried. So I let her down pretty quick, for I did not want to play with her if she was going to be such a baby, and she ran off to the barn."

"And you have not seen her since?"

"Why, no, grandmamma," said Cosmo, beginning to feel a little ashamed as he thought over the occurrence, "you see I wanted to feed Whitefoot."

"Ah! I'm afraid, my boy, that you have forgotten that because Ettie is a girl and not as strong as you, you ought to treat her with so much the more consideration. It is cowardly to oppress the weak."

"But I did not mean to oppress her."

"That was oppression to keep her up in the air on the see-saw, when you knew she could not get down."

"Well, she need not have cried."

"Perhaps it was not the wisest thing to do, but then that does not alter your conduct. But here we are at the kitchen-door—go in and ask Sophy for a basket, and after you have picked the corn you can come and tell me if you do not think I am right."

Cosmo obeyed, for to tell the truth, he was rather glad to escape from one of his grandmamma's plain talks; they made him feel too sensibly that he was in the wrong. It did not take him very long to pick the corn for dinner, and as he left the garden he said to himself: "I suppose I may as well tell grandmamma I was in the wrong, for I know that I was, and then if I go and make up with Ettie it will be off my mind, for she is a nice little girl when she don't cry."

So leaving his corn in the kitchen, he went to find his grandmamma. She was in her room, and when he told her that he was sorry, she kissed him very warmly, and said that she hoped he and Ettie would have no more disputes, while they were together.

Then he went off to find Ettie, but he went to the wrong field, and so he missed her, and just as he was going in search of her he heard the horn for dinner, and supposing he should meet her on the way, he hastened home; but she was there first, and as they were all assembling at the table, he did not like to say any thing to her about the occurrence of the morning then. She seemed to have got over any unkind feelings that she might have had, and talked very pleasantly to Cosmo, as well as to her grandparents. As they rose from the table and Ettie went out on the piazza, Cosmo followed her, and proposed to her to go blackberrying.

"I thought you did not like to play with girls," replied Ettie, smiling.

Cosmo blushed as he said: "I am sorry I

said that this morning, and teased you so. I
don't mean to do it again if I can help it."

"That's right, my boy," said his grandfather, who had been standing unobserved by
the window, and had heard what he said;
"never be ashamed to confess yourself in the
wrong when you are, or to say that you are
sorry; that is truly manly. But who is
this?" he continued, as a wagon stopped at
the gate, and a little boy about Cosmo's size
jumped out and ran up the path to the house.

"Why, it is James Ford!" exclaimed
Cosmo, "and he is going to stay too, for see
the wagon is driving off," and he ran to
meet him with great delight.

Mr. Linton received him with much kindness, for he knew him to be a good boy, and
he was pleased too to see that he seemed glad
to see Ettie there.

"Do you like to play with girls, James?"
said Mrs. Linton, as she introduced Ettie to
him.

"Oh! yes, ma'am, I play a great deal with my sister Mattie, and she is just about as large as Ettie."

Ettie had felt a little disappointed when she saw James come in, for she thought that now Cosmo would not care to play with her, and the blackberrying would have to be given up; but when she heard James speak so pleasantly, she changed her mind and was glad that he had come.

"The children were just going up on the hill to pick blackberries," said their grand-mamma, guessing what was in Ettie's thoughts, "can't you go with them, James."

He seemed quite pleased at the plan.

"My father is coming back for me in about an hour," said he, "and we can pick a good many blackberries in that time. He told me to ask you if Cosmo could not come to see me to-morrow. There is a nice woods near the mill, where Mattie and I often have pic-nics, and in one corner of it there is a natural oven where we make a fire, and roast corn

and potatoes.   We want to have a pic-nic to-
morrow, and if Ettie can come, Mattie will be
glad to see her."

Ettie and Cosmo looked eagerly at their
grandfather, hoping he would say yes.   But
he hesitated a little about giving his consent.

"I am very willing," said he, "that they
should come to see you and Mattie, but I
don't know about the fire."

"Oh! there is no danger, I assure you,
Mr. Linton," said James, "and if you ask my
father he will tell you so."

"Very well, I will see him when he comes
for you, and if he says it is quite safe, per
haps I may consent.   In the mean time you
may go and enjoy yourselves on the hill
among the blackberry bushes."

Only half-satisfied with this conditional
promise, the children took the pails which
their grandmamma gave them—there was
one for James too—and started for the hill.
They crossed the brook where Cosmo fished,
James helping Ettie over as if he had been

used to taking care of girls. As they passed through the lot which had been the scene of Cosmo's first haying, he remembered how uncomfortable he had felt at Jerry's teasing, and made up his mind not to tease Ettie again at any rate.

After they crossed the lot they entered a little thicket of bushes, and there the blackberries grew in profusion. It was called the hill, though in reality the ground did not rise much until they passed through this thicket, so the blackberries might be said to grow at the foot of the hill rather than on the hill. Ettie had never seen so many blackberries together before, and she did not know where to begin picking first, but James found her a good place, and they were all soon busily filling their pails. James held the bushes back for Ettie, and Cosmo tried to follow his example. Once or twice the thought came in his mind that it would be good fun to frighten Ettie by telling her of the hornets' nest, and how he was stung, or by talking of snakes, but he remembered his resolution not to tease her, so he said nothing about it.

Their pails were quite small, so it did not take the children long to fill them, particularly as the berries were so numerous and large, and when they were filled Cosmo proposed that they should climb to the top of the hill and see the village. So leaving their pails behind a large stone, they clambered up the hill. It was not very high, but there was quite an extensive prospect from its summit. In the distance the spire of the village church could be seen, with the houses clustered about it, and the road winding towards James' home. As they were trying to see if they could distinguish the mill, James spied a wagon coming along the road.

"Oh! there's my father!" exclaimed he; "let us hurry and we will reach the house as soon as he does."

"Now for a race down the hill," said Cosmo, "one, two, three, and away," and off he started, with James by his side. Ettie started

to run too, but the hill was pretty steep, and
she had only run a few steps when her foot
tripped and down she fell. She would have
rolled all the way down if she had not caught
a bush and thus saved herself. She was not
hurt much, but was a good deal frightened,
and cried very loudly. Both the boys hastened to her, Cosmo half-inclined to call her
a baby, but when he saw James help her up
so carefully, and ask her if she was much
hurt so kindly, he followed his example, and
between them they helped her down the hill.
She had quite recovered from her fright, and
her tears were all dry when they reached the
stone where they had left their berries. They
did not get to the house before Mr. Ford,
though, for when they came down the lane
they saw his wagon standing by the gate, and
Mr. Linton talking to him.

" Well, young folks," said he, as the children came up, " you have been berrying, I
hear ; have you picked many ?"

" Oh ! yes, sir," said Cosmo, displaying his

pailful, "and James has just as many to take home for his supper."

"Well, your grandpapa says that you may come to-morrow and have a pic-nic with James, so come as early you can."

"Oh! may we go, grandpapa," said both the children at once; "how glad I am," and James looked as pleased as they did.

"Yes, Mr. Ford assures me there is no danger, and that he can see you all the time from the mill, so I am going to take you down in the wagon to-morrow morning."

By this time James was seated by his father, with his pail of berries in his hand, and so after again urging the children to come early, they drove off.

The children had their berries for tea, and enjoyed them very much, for their walk had given them an appetite. They had plenty to tell of their afternoon's adventures too—how Ettie fell down, and how Cosmo picked her up.

"Did you show Ettie the place where the

hornets' nest was, Cosmo?" asked his grand-mother.

"No, I did not, for I thought it might make her afraid to go among the bushes."

His grandmother gave him an approving nod and smile, and Ettie asked what hornets' nest. Then Cosmo told her about his being stung, and how Caleb burnt up the nest.

"Oh! how I wish I had been here to see it," said Ettie. "Never mind, we shall see a fire to-morrow; will you give us some corn and potatoes to roast, grandpapa?"

"Yes, you shall have all you want, but go to bed now, or else you will be too sleepy to wake up in the morning." So with a good night kiss the children went up to bed.

CHAPTER VIII

The next morning was pleasant, to the great joy of the children, and as soon as breakfast was over, the wagon came to the door. Grandmamma had a basket containing bread and butter and four little pies for their picnic, and grandpapa came in from the garden with a basket full of corn and potatoes. "You can roast as much as you want," said he, as he put the basket in the wagon; "and give what is left to James to take to his mother."

"Oh!" said Cosmo as they were all seated in the wagon ready for a start; "I have forgotten a cup to drink out of." He was just going to get out again, when Abby brought him one. He put it in the basket, and off they drove.

Cosmo had to share the pleasure of driving with Ettie, to whom his grandpapa gave the reins, saying: "There, let me see if you can drive as well as your mother."

"Why, do girls ever drive?" said Cosmo.

"To be sure they do," replied his grandfather; "there is many a lady round here who can drive as well as I can, and I never used to be afraid to let Ettie's mother drive any where."

Ettie seemed to like holding the reins very well, but when she saw that Cosmo was impatient for his turn, she gave them up to him, and he drove until they reached the mill.

James and Mattie were waiting for them; and they too, had a basket of good things for their pic-nic, but no corn, for Mr. Linton had said he must provide that.

The place which the children had chosen for their pic-nic ground was indeed beautiful. It was a fine grove of trees, just by the side of the mill-pond. In the farthest corner, away from the trees, was what James called his oven. It was formed of several small rocks close together, leaving a hollow place in the centre, in which he had placed a flat stone, on which he made his fire.

Mr. Linton went with the children to see this oven, and to satisfy himself that no danger could arise from the fire. He saw that with a moderate degree of carefulness there could be no fear of their getting hurt; so after cautioning Ettie not to go very near, as her clothes might burn very easily, he drove off, telling the children that he would return for them at three o'clock.

They immediately set to work gathering dried leaves and sticks to make their fire with. They found an abundance scattered about the grove; when they had collected quite a heap of fuel, James built the fire all ready for lighting. First he put in some dried leaves, then some small sticks, and on the top of all, a large stick which he had brought from home. Then he felt in his pockets for matches, but he had forgotten them. Mattie was ready to go for them; she thought her father had some at the mill. She was right, and he gave her some, so she was only gone a few minutes.

Cosmo wanted to put the corn right on to roast as soon as the fire commenced to burn, but James told him that would not do, it would get smoked if he did. They must wait until the fire burned very well, and there were some coals, before the corn or potatoes would roast. So the children stood watching the flames, Ettie at a little distance, as her grandfather had told her to do. It was a good time for the little girls to make acquaintance with each other, and Mattie began by showing her little visitor the house where she lived, one end of which could be seen through the trees; and then Ettie said she lived in a town and had never been in the country much, but she liked it, and that she would rather play all day in the woods than with the handsomest baby-house she saw.

13

"Have you got a baby-house, Mattie?" Ettie asked.

"Why, sometimes I make one out here on the rocks," was her reply. "I use leaves for plates, and acorns for saucers, and I find shining stones by the pond to make my house look pretty."

"That must be nice," said Ettie. "I think I should like it better than my baby-house which has three rooms in it, all furnished." And she was going on to describe it when the boys called to them that they were going to roast the corn and potatoes now, so they went to see them do it. The husks had been taken off the ears, and James placed them in the oven, not directly on the coals, but leaning against the side of the rock, so that the heat of the fire would cook them without burning them. He put in four ears, one for each of them, and when they were done, he said he would roast the potatoes. It did not take the corn very long to cook, and the children had hardly time to get impatient before James drew it out so smoking hot, that it almost burnt his fingers. Mattie's mother had given her a clean, brown towel, which she spread on one of the rocks, to receive the corn as James drew it out.

"Now for the potatoes," said he; and Cosmo handed him several, which he placed on the coals.

"I suppose the corn is too hot to eat yet, and besides we want salt to sprinkle on it, and I forgot to bring any. Have you some, Cosmo?"

"No," Cosmo said he did not know there was any needed.

"Never mind," said Mattie; "I will run to the house for some."

"Do, that's a good girl," said James; "while I roast these potatoes."

So Mattie ran off as glad as most sisters are to do any thing for their brothers, though to do James justice, he did not often send her for things which he could get himself, only this time he could not leave his fire.

By the time Mattie returned, the corn was quite cool enough to eat, and the children thought they had never tasted any so nice. Grandmamma's bread and butter was good too. The pies and cakes in Mattie's basket they kept for dessert, to eat after they had eaten the potatoes. They took longer to roast than the corn had done, but the children took turns watching them, while the others played tag among the trees.

But when they were roasted there arose a difficulty, which was, how to get them out. They were too near the coals for James to take them with his fingers without burning them. Mattie proposed to go to the house for a pair of tongs.

"I'll tell you," said James, after a moment's consideration. "I'll make a pair of tongs out of these sticks." So he chose two nice stout sticks, and made them flat at one end with his knife. Then he took one in each hand, and placing one on each side of a

potato, he drew them out one by one
"There," said he when he had laid them
all on the rock, "is not that a good pair
of tongs, only they are not joined together?"
The children all agreed that it was, and
Cosmo secretly wished that he knew as much
as James Ford.   Perhaps he knew more
than James of what can be learned from
books, but boys who have lived all their
lives in the country, generally have more of
what is called contrivance than city boys.

The potatoes proved to be quite as good
as the corn, and the pies, one for each of the
children, were pronounced to be grandmamma's best.   Ettie proposed that they
should save the cakes until by and by, when
they could have a tea-party; to this they all
agreed, so James covered up the fire, saying
they might want to roast some more corn
then, while the others placed the baskets all
together by the rock; and Mattie, like a
neat housewife, gathered up the corn-husks

13*

and cobs, and potato-skins, saying — "I know a little grunter who will like these," which made Ettie laugh.

James said there was a beautiful walk up above the mill, along the borders of the stream which turned the wheel, so they all started in that direction. Ettie and Mattie, who felt as if they had known each other all their lives, with their arms around each other's waists, walked together, talking very confidentially about their dolls, and their schools and homes. The boys strolled on ahead, now and then stopping to throw stones in the water or to watch the squirrels jump from branch to branch.

"How I should like to have a squirrel to take home with me," said Cosmo. "I might buy him a house with my half-dollar, and I could teach him to eat out of my hand just as Whitefoot does." And Cosmo went on, forming plans where he should keep his squirrel, and what he would give him to eat, just as if the squirrel had been in his hands instead of jumping about on the tree.

"Yes, but you have got to catch your squirrel first," said James; "and that may not be as easy as you think, for they are nimble little fellows."

"Oh! no fear but that I can catch one," said Cosmo, who meant to show James Ford that he could do something. "I can climb any tree there is here in this woods. There's a squirrel now," he continued, "just running up that tree; ah! my fine fellow, I am after you." And throwing off his jacket, he began to climb the tree. It was a pretty little red fellow, and as he ran nimbly up the tree, the children admired him very much. Cosmo had been practising climbing trees ever since he had come to his grandfather's, so he had no difficulty in climbing this one. The squirrel, as if conscious that he had the advantage of his pursuer, ran to the end of one of the limbs, and there rested, as much as to say: "Here I am safe."

But Cosmo was too intent upon catching his prize to notice that the limb, which projected far out over the stream, was not strong enough to bear his weight; so he crept softly along, hat in hand, ready to throw it over the squirrel, thinking he was sure of him now. James had hardly time to call out, "Cosmo, you'll fall," when the limb cracked, and splash went Cosmo, right into the water, while the squirrel, who had jumped to another limb as soon as he heard the crack, was no doubt laughing at the fine escape he had made.

The children did not feel much like laughing, though. Ettie especially, was very much frightened, for she thought Cosmo would be drowned. But James knew that the water was not deep enough for that. His fear was that he might be carried, by the force of the water, over the dam before he could get out. But they were a good distance up the stream, so the water did not run very rapidly, and he was only carried a few paces before he regained his footing and waded to the shore. He felt rather forlorn as he stepped on the grass, with the water dripping from his clothes, and somewhat mortified at his ill-success after all his boasting. But James was very considerate, and did not laugh at him, while the little girls were too much frightened to think of such a thing.

"O Cosmo! what will you do?" said Ettie, "you are so wet, and grandpapa is not coming for us until three o'clock!"

"Why," said James, "he will have to come to our house and put on some of my clothes. To be sure they will be rather large for him; but here's his jacket, which fortunately is not wet, and it is no matter if the other things do not fit so very well. But what's the matter?" he continued, as he noticed that Cosmo limped a little.

"I think I turned my foot in trying to save myself when the limb broke," said

Cosmo, "and it hurts me some to walk; but I guess it will be better after I use it a little."

The children walked slowly back, quite a contrast to the merry party which had left the grove but a short time before. Just before they reached the mill, there was a bridge over the stream which they had to cross to go to Mr. Ford's house, which was on the opposite side of the stream from the mill. James led Cosmo across while Mattie and Ettie went to tell Mr. Ford of the accident.

When the boys reached the house they were met by James' mother, who expressed much concern at the mishap, and hoped there would be no more serious consequences arising from it than a ducking. She told James to take Cosmo to his room and give him a dry suit of clothes, and she gave him something to bathe his foot with.

The boys had a good laugh at the long trowsers and shirt-sleeves: they covered

Cosmo's feet and hands; but after turning them up, and putting on his own jacket, they did not look so badly, and they felt so comfortable after wearing his wet clothes so long, that he almost forget his lame foot. It did not pain him nearly so much after it was rub'sed with Mrs. Ford's liniment, and James' shoes were easy for his feet, so he proposed that now they should go and have their tea-party, and roast some more corn.

When they arrived at the grove, they found the girls had got there before them, and were busily setting a table, as they said. They had chosen a large rock for their table, and large maple leaves for plates. Ettie had taken the cup from the basket, and had filled it with water from a spring which Mattie had shown to her. This she placed in the centre of the table, surrounded by Mrs. Ford's cakes.

James found that his fire had not gone out, so he added a few sticks, and he was soon ready to roast the corn; this time he put in six ears, for he said: "Perhaps father and

Mr. Linton may like to eat one." Mr. Linton's wagon drove down the lane just as the corn was roasted, and after tying his horse, he came with Mr. Ford to the grove.

"What! eating yet?" he exclaimed, as he saw James taking the corn from the oven, "it seems to me you have great appetites."

"O grandpapa!" said Ettie, laughing; "we have not been eating all the time: we finished our dinner long ago, and now we are taking our tea; and we have an ear of corn for you and for Mr. Ford."

Her grandfather took the ear which James handed to him, and then let it drop suddenly as if it had burnt his hands, though he was only in fun; but the children were greatly amused. However, he ate it as if he thought it very good.

Cosmo, all this time had kept pretty still, almost dreading to have his grandpapa know of his foolishness in attempting to catch a squirrel by climbing a tree after him. But after a while Mr. Linton noticed his clothes:

"Why, Cosmo!" said he, "your clothes seem suddenly to have stretched and become too large for you!"

"Oh!" said Ettie, glad to tell the story over again, "those are James Ford's clothes; Cosmo got his all wet when he fell into the brook trying to catch a squirrel!"

"Why, did he go into a brook after a squirrel? I thought that squirrels lived in trees, not in the water."

"Well, but grandpapa, he was trying to catch it on a tree—only the limb broke, and so he fell into the water."

"Oh! now I understand," said his grandpapa, "but I hope you did not hurt yourself, my boy?"

"No, sir; I only turned my foot a little."

"Did you? why, I'm sorry for that; but I guess a little of grandmamma's rubbing will cure it; and if you have finished your tea-party I think we will start for home."

James ran to the house for Cosmo's clothes, while Ettie and Mattie gathered up the

14

baskets and cleared up the dining-room, they said. Then Mr. Linton helped the children into the wagon, for Cosmo found that his foot hurt him a good deal when he attempted to jump into the wagon; and by the time they were comfortably seated, James returned with the clothes, which had been dried by the kitchen fire.

The children then bade each other good-by; Cosmo and Ettie declaring they had had a very pleasant day, notwithstanding the tumble into the brook.

Ettie had a great deal to tell her grand-papa of the fine fun they had, and how good the corn and potatoes, and grandmamma's pie, had tasted; but Cosmo was very silent, for, to tell the truth, his foot pained him very much, and he was thinking, too, that it was all caused by his self-confidence.

But after he had got home, and his grand-mamma had rubbed it, it felt so much better that he was able to go out to feed Whitefoot, and see-saw with Ettie. And when he went

to bed he thought it would be all well the next day.

He was mistaken, however; the next morning his foot and ankle were so much swollen, that his grandfather sent for the village doctor. He said, after examining it, that it was a slight sprain, but he must keep very quiet for two or three days, or he might be lame a good while.

Poor Cosmo! it was pretty hard for him to keep still; he had been so used, during these weeks that he had spent at his grandfather's, to being out of doors all the time that he felt the confinement more than he would have done at home. Still it was not quite as bad as if Ettie had not been there. She devoted herself to his amusement, reading to him, telling him stories, and playing games with him as he sat with his lame foot up on the sofa. She scarcely went out at all and when, on the second day of his lameness, her grandpapa proposed to take her with him to the village, she said she would rather not leave Cosmo. But her cousin would not consent to that.

"No, no, Ettie," said he, "I don't want you to stay in the house with me all the time; you must go for a ride, and I will read and paint while you are gone."

She accordingly went with her grandpapa, leaving Cosmo with an interesting book to read, and a little table with his paint-box and drawing - paper, when he was tired of reading.

Ettie's unselfishness and kindness to him had a great effect on Cosmo, and he began to think more of girls than he had before. He even told his grandmamma when she came with her knitting to sit by him, that he thought girls were very good company when a fellow was sick and unable to go out.

When his cousin came home, she brought him a new book, and had many things to tell him. She had seen James and Mattie at the village, and they had inquired about him

"And, O Cosmo!" said she, "I saw some calves in a field, and one was almost exactly like Whitefoot, only instead of the brown spot being on its forehead, it was on its back."

"Then I am sure it was not as pretty," said Cosmo. "Dear little Whitefoot, how glad I shall be to see her." At this, Ettie smiled, and ran up to her grandfather and whispered something to him, and he replied: "Perhaps so to-morrow morning." Cosmo wondered what she said, but he did not ask any questions.

"And now," continued Ettie, "I have got the best thing of all," and she laid a letter on his table. It was to Cosmo from his mother, and oh! how glad he was to get it. It was full of love and news. They all wanted him home again very much, and Margaret hoped that he would not burn any more hornets' nests, for she was so much afraid he would get hurt.

"Dear Margaret," said Cosmo, "I suppose

if she knew that I was lame now, she would start off to-morrow to take care of me."

His mother said that Ettie's papa could not go home as soon as he had intended, so that Ettie was to stay at her grandpapa's as long as Cosmo did, and return home with him. This was good news to them all, and the children began immediately to plan what they would do while they staid.

Cosmo could not help wondering after he went to bed, what it was that Ettie whispered to his grandpapa, but he did not find out until after breakfast the next morning. Then he was lying on the sofa all alone, wondering where Ettie could be, when he heard her voice in the kitchen, and soon a patter of feet in the passage which led to the dining-room, very different from any which he had ever heard in the house before. He looked towards the door which was partly open, and there he saw Whitefoot's face peeping in.

"Why, Whitefoot," he exclaimed, "how

did you get here? come here, old pet, and let
me see you."

She knew his voice, and coming up to
him licked the hand which he put out to pat
her. She had a wreath of flowers round her
neck, and looked as proud as a calf might be
supposed to look, with so much finery on.
She did not seem at all bashful, but acted as
much at home in the dining-room as in the
orchard, though she had never been in the
house before. "But how did you get in,
Whitefoot, tell me that?" said Cosmo, as he
stroked her head.

Just then, he heard Ettie's merry laugh
behind the door. "Ah! now I know," said
he, "Ettie brought you in, and that was what
she whispered to grandpapa last night. I am
sure I am very glad to see you."

Then Ettie came in, her face full of smiles,
and told how she had put the flowers round
the calf's neck, and then coaxed her in by
showing her some salt. She gave some to
Cosmo to feed her with, and then she got a
piece of cake to see if she would eat that.

Whitefoot ate it as eagerly as any little child would, and then grandmamma came in and thought she had been in the house long enough, so Ettie took her back to the orchard.

That day Cosmo could walk about the house with very little pain, and he was very anxious to pay a visit to the orchard, and barn, and garden; but his grandmamma advised him not to try walking out of doors, for he might increase his lameness so that he would have to keep quite still.

So he tried to follow her advice and be patient, though it was rather hard work. In the morning his grandmother let him come with Ettie into the kitchen and see her make cake. Cosmo grated the nutmeg, and Ettie beat the eggs, and they thought that they helped a great deal.

Then Cosmo wrote a letter to his mother, and after dinner Ettie cut out paper dolls, and Cosmo painted them; so after all, he had quite a pleasant day.

CHAPTER IX

When Cosmo was again able to go out and play, he was much more inclined to treat Ettie with consideration than he had been before his accident. James Ford's example had had some effect upon him; but the chief cause of the change was Ettie's patient devotion to him while he was lame. He was sure that he could not have given up his out-of-door amusements, so pleasantly to stay with her if she had been in his place, and he was obliged to confess that in that, she was far superior to him if she was a girl.

So when they went to play in the orchard again, he was quite ready to let her have her turn first, when his grandpa or Jerry could swing them, or swing her himself when they were not there, though he knew that she was not strong enough to swing him in return. He was willing to stop the see-saw whenever she was tired, and even to admire and notice the kittens quite as much as she wished him to do.

To tell the truth, the kittens were much more deserving of admiration now than when Ettie first found them, for they could open their eyes and look at the children when they went to visit them, and they began to play a little.

Cosmo would not allow that they were half as interesting as Whitefoot, though. She certainly was a very wonderfully wise and affectionate calf; even Ettie acknowledged that Cosmo was right in preferring her to the kittens.

But Whitefoot had her faults as well as some other animals, and one day she gave Cosmo a great fright, besides a good deal of amusement after it was all over.

It was only a day or two after Cosmo's foot had got well. He and Ettie were playing in the orchard, when they heard Caleb calling them. He had come from the field just beyond the barn, and was holding something in his hand, which he wished to show them.

"It's a snake, Ettie," said Cosmo, as Caleb held it up, "come quick and see it;" and without waiting to shut the gate, he ran as fast as he could, and Ettie after him.

Whitefoot, seeing the gate open, and not being tied, did not see why she should not go too; so she followed the children, but instead of going up to the barn as they did, she crossed the lane, and finding the gate open to the path which led to the kitchen, she went in there. Then remembering, no doubt, the fine treat she had had, when she was in the house before, she concluded to walk in. There was no one in the kitchen, for Mrs. Linton was busy in her own room, Abby was in the cellar, and Sophy in the garden; so she walked on to the dining-room. No one was there either, but having a good deal of curiosity, and seeing a door on one side

of the dining-room open, she went to see
what was there.   It happened to be the
pantry - door, which Cosmo had left open
when he went to get some cake for himself
and Ettie to eat in the orchard.   What was
of more consequence to Whitefoot, he had
also left the cake-pot uncovered.   She helped
herself to this without delay, and was having
a fine repast, when Abby came into the
dining - room.   "There," said she, "those
children have left that pantry-door open, and
the place will be full of flies;" so she slammed
it shut hastily, without noticing Whitefoot,
who was partly behind the door and had her
nose deep in the cake-pot.

In the mean time, Cosmo and Ettie had
examined and wondered at Caleb's snake,
quite as much as he desired.   It was one
which he had killed in crossing a marshy
field that morning, when he was looking for
a cow which had been lost, and was larger
than they had ever seen before.   Then
they returned to the orchard to eat the cake,

which they had left in a little basket hanging on one of the lower limbs of an apple-tree.

"Let us see if Whitefoot likes cake as well as she did the other day," said Ettie, as she took her piece from the basket.

"Well," said Cosmo, and he called "Whitefoot! Whitefoot!" but no Whitefoot came. He looked around to see why she did not come. "Why, where can she be?" he said, as he saw no signs of her little white face. He ran to the farther end of the orchard, but she was no where to be found.

"She must have gone out when we did, for I forgot to shut the gate—O Ettie! if she should be lost," and Cosmo's heart sank within him at the thought.

"Oh! she can not be lost, she must have followed us to the barn without our noticing her. We were so taken up with looking at the snake; let us go and see if she is there."

So leaving their basket, cake and all on

15

the ground, they hurried to the barn, calling "Whitefoot! Whitefoot!" as loud as they could. They looked in every corner of the barn and barn-yard, and they called so loudly, that the hens thought they ought to help them, so they cackled as loud as they could; while old puss, who thought they must want her, though they called her by a new name, jumped out of her box and came running to them. But Ettie was too much excited to stop, even to pat pussy; so leaving her to wonder at this strange behavior, they went on to the field where Caleb and their grandfather were cutting down grain.

"Oh! have you seen any thing of Whitefoot?" they both exclaimed.

"What, has Whitefoot gone?" said their grandfather.

"Yes, I left the gate open," said Cosmo, "when I went to see the snake, and when we went back she was gone. We have looked all about the barn, but she is not there."

"If she had come this way we should have seen her," said his grandfather; "perhaps she went towards the road instead of following you. I will come and help you look for her." And he followed the children out of the field, hardly able to keep pace with their eager footsteps.

They passed the barn again and the orchard, and went down the lane towards the road, but the gate opening into the road was shut, and Cosmo did not think it had been opened that morning.

"Oh! dear, if we should never find her," said he, "my pretty Whitefoot!"

"Oh! we shall find her," said his grandfather, "may be she is in the garden."

Animated with this new hope, Cosmo began to call "Whitefoot!" louder than ever, as he turned his steps towards the garden. As he was passing the house, he thought he heard an answering bleat. He listened—it was Whitefoot's voice, but where did it come from? He could not see her any where.

"There she is! there she is!" exclaimed
Ettie, laughing so she could hardly stand
up.

"Where?" said Cosmo.

"Why, there, look, look!" screamed Ettie
pointing to the house.

Cosmo looked, and so did his grandfather,
and they both laughed as loud as Ettie, until
Abby and Sophy came to see what was
the matter, when they both held up their
hands in astonishment, for there, out of the
little window of the pantry, was Whitefoot's
head, as if in a frame, and she looking as
innocent as though she had not eaten all the
cake out of grandma's cake-pot.

"Why, how could she have got in there?"
said every body at once.

"Why, I will tell you," said grandma who
had now joined the group of spectators, and
was as much amused as any of them. "She
liked her visit to the dining-room so much
the other day, that she thought she would

repeat it, only this time she has got a little further, and has gone into the pantry."

"I wonder if she was there when I shut the pantry-door," said Abby, as they all went in to let the calf out.

"Very likely," said Mrs. Linton, "for here is the door shut, and when she heard Cosmo call, she pushed the window-shutter open, trying to get out in that way. When you shut the door she was probably behind it, for here is the cake-pot."

"Yes," said Sophy, "and as I live, not a crumb of cake left.   O Cosmo! this is all your doings."

Cosmo who had led Whitefoot out of the pantry and stood caressing her, looked a little guilty, as he said :

"I know, grandma, that I ought to have covered the cake-pot, and shut the door, but I was in such a hurry that I forgot."

"Well, try and remember the next time," said his grandmother, "and there is no great harm done, only you will have to go without

15*

cake for tea to-night, for it is too late to make any to-day, and you and Ettie will have to help me make some more to-morrow."

Cosmo was very grateful to his kind grandmamma, that she did not seem displeased with him, and he kissed her over and over again.

But she was like all grandmammas, very forbearing and considerate to her grandchildren, for it was no slight thing for Mrs. Linton, so fond of order as she was, to have a calf shut up for half the morning in her neat pantry.

"Of one thing we may be certain," said Cosmo's grandfather, as he led Whitefoot away. "Your calf has good taste, to like your grandmamma's cake; fortunately it was not very rich, or it might have made her sick."

But Whitefoot seemed as well and as lively after her visit to the pantry as before. Though I am not sure but she ate the cake which Cosmo and Ettie dropped on the ground when they went to look for her, besides emptying the cake-pot, yet she was not sick. Perhaps it was because she ran so many races with Cosmo around the orchard. Sometimes it seemed as if she really understood how to play "tag," for when Cosmo and Ettie ran after each other, dodging around the trees, she ran too, and they had hard work to catch her.

"Let me see," said Ettie's grandfather, at the dinner-table, the day they found White-foot in the pantry, "I think I shall have to give Ettie a calf too, and see if she can not teach it better manners than to steal her grandmamma's cake."

"Oh! if you please, grandpapa, I would rather have a chicken," said Ettie, "for I am sure I could never make either of the other calves as tame as Whitefoot."

"Well, then, how would you like the white hen? she has just brought out a brood of chickens."

"Oh! I should like that so much! and I

can call her 'Lily;' that's what I wanted Cosmo to call his calf."

"I'm afraid the chickens will not amount to much, they are hatched so late," said her grandmamma.

"Oh! no matter, said Mr. Linton, "some of them will live and be just ready to roast when Ettie comes here next summer."

"O grandpapa! I should not like to have any of them killed!" said the little girl, glancing ruefully at the chickens which her grandfather was carving, "I wish we needn't to eat animals."

"Why, child, that is what they were given to us for; but don't be alarmed, we will not kill any of your chickens until you say that we may; but you shall have all their eggs. In the mean time as you had no particular acquaintance with these chickens, and no great affection for them when they were alive, I hope you will not object to eating some of them now, and to picking this wish-bone."

Ettie consented to eat the chicken in consideration of having the wish-bone, which she said was so large that it would make a capital black cook.

"A black cook!" said Cosmo, looking up in surprise, "what do you mean?"

"Oh! you'll see," said Ettie, laughing. "I'll make her this evening if grandmamma will give me some black sealing-wax."

Cosmo looked more puzzled than ever, but there was nothing to do but to wait and see what Ettie meant. He did not know much about girls' contrivances.

"Perhaps she thinks Whitefoot will need a cook to make her cake—she eats it so fast!" said his grandfather, smiling.

After dinner they went out to see "Lily," as Ettie already called her new pet. They found her in a very comfortable coop, surrounded by a brood of little chickens, for whom she was trying to pick up as good a living as the limited space around her could afford; it is my opinion that she would not

have succeeded very well if Ettie had not
helped her by providing her with plenty of
meal and water. She did not seem very
much affected by the news, when Ettie told
her that she was hers now ; but when Ettie
tried to catch one of her little brood, she
clucked and bristled out her feathers in a
most alarming manner.

That evening Ettie kept her promise and
showed Cosmo how to make the black cook.
She melted some black sealing-wax which
her grandmamma gave her, and covered the
top of the bone with it; while it was soft, she
formed it into a round head, and made something like a nose on it. Then she stuck in
two little white beads for eyes, and put on
some red sealing-wax for a mouth. She
stuck on some black sealing-wax, too, for
feet. Her grandmamma gave her some red
flannel, with which she made a cloak to cover
the thin legs of her cook—if she had any
arms, they were hid by her cloak.

Cosmo watched Ettie make this with much

interest; and he concluded that she was a genius, for it was almost as hard to make as a kite.

"I wonder if Mattie Ford knows how to make these cooks," said Ettie. "I mean to ask her the next time I see her, and if she don't I'll give her this one."

CHAPTER X

Ettie did not have to wait very long to ask Mattie about the black cook, for the very next morning her father, finding that he had business which would take him past Mr. Linton's house, had offered to leave her there, while he attended to it, and call for her again on his return home.

Mattie was of course delighted at this prospect of seeing her friend Ettie, so she lost no time in getting ready and going to tell James about it. He was pleased to see her so happy, yet he could not help wishing that he was going too. His father read this in his face, as he stood by the gate to see them drive off.

"Why, what's the reason you can not go, too, James?" said he; "we can make room for you here among the meal-bags, you don't mind getting a little whitened, I suppose, as you are a miller's son?"

"Oh! no, father, I don't mind that! and I should like to go very much indeed."

"Well, jump in then, and take your fishing-pole too, as you have it in your hand, and may be you and Cosmo can catch some fish in Mr. Linton's brook."

James did not wait for a second invitation, but was in among the meal-bags almost before his father had finished speaking. Mattie, who sat on the seat with her father, kept looking behind at him, as they drove along, and laughing at the droll appearance he made.

Ettie and Cosmo gave them a very warm welcome, and Cosmo was not long in getting his fishing-rod, and leading the way to the brook, where he and James had a very pleasant morning together.

The little girls staid in the orchard, and had a pleasant quiet play together there. Ettie brought out her doll, which had been sleeping in her trunk ever since she left home, for she had had so many other amusements that she had not cared to play with her. Besides, she knew that Cosmo would not care to take any notice of dolls.

Mattie admired her very much, and Ettie let her be the mamma all the time she staid. She showed Mattie how to make paper-dolls too, and gave her some patterns. And as for the black cook, Mattie thought she had never seen any thing so funny. She was delighted when Ettie gave it to her, and she said that she meant to make plenty of them next winter. Then in her turn she showed Ettie how to make babies with walnut heads. Ettie's grandmamma gave her some nuts for the purpose. Thus the morning had almost passed away before Ettie thought of showing the kittens.

"O Mattie!" she exclaimed, as soon as she thought of them, "don't you want to see our kittens?"

Of course Mattie loved kittens, as all little

girls do, so away they ran to the barn, taking Miss Dollie, the black cook, the walnut babies, and the paper dolls with them. Mrs. Puss did not know what to make of so many visitors, but she tried to purr them as loud a welcome as she could, while the kittens were as playful as possible.

"Oh! what little darlings they are," said Mattie, "that little gray one is just like the one I lost last winter!"

"Did you lose a kitten?"

"Yes; she followed me one day when I went for a walk, and I never saw her afterwards; she must have wandered from me into the woods, though I never knew what became of her."

"And have you no kitten now?"

"No, I have never had any since then."

"I wish you would take this little gray one, then," said Ettie; "for grandmamma said, the other day, that she would like to give away one or two of these kittens, and I would rather you had them than any body else."

Mattie's eyes sparkled with pleasure at this, and she thought as she looked at the kitten, it was even prettier than the one she had lost.

Away went the two little girls to ask Mrs. Linton about it. She was very glad to have Mattie take the kitten, and she gave them a nice little basket to put it in. Back again they trudged to the barn, without seeming to think whether their little feet were tired or not, and proceeded to put kitty in her new habitation, after having first lined it with hay.

It was well old puss was not there, for I do not know what she would have said to see her beloved child shut up in that dark prison, and to hear her piteous mewing.

As for her little brothers and sister, they did nothing but peep over the top of their box to see what it was all about, and then tumble backwards, for fun I suppose.

By the time kitty was safely conveyed to the house, Mr. Ford drove up to the gate to take his children home. But Mr. Linton was just coming in to dinner, and it was all . on the table, and it would be a shame to let the children go away hungry, so he must tie his horse, and come in to dinner too.

This was what Mrs. Linton said, as she came out to urge him to stay. There was no resisting so many good reasons, so Mr. Ford came in, followed by James and Cosmo, who had returned from fishing a short time before, in great good-humor at their success. They had been further up the stream than Cosmo had ever been alone, and had found an abundance of fish.

As for Ettie and Mattie, they were so much engaged in trying to make the kitten lap a saucer of milk, that they could hardly be persuaded to eat their own dinner at all. Kitty proved a pretty apt scholar, though—besides, she was hungry, so the saucer of milk soon disappeared; and Mattie, having finished her own dinner, the little creature was again imprisoned in the basket, and after

16*

many kind words, Mr. Ford and his children drove off.

Kitty did not enjoy her ride very much, and she thought at first, that she could never be contented in her new home away from all her relations and old friends. But Mattie petted her so much, and seemed to love her so dearly, that after a while she recovered her spirits and became as playful as ever.

About this time Cosmo wrote another letter home, telling his mother about his rides on horseback, but as he got tired of writing and did not tell his mother so much as you would like to know perhaps, I think I will tell you about them myself instead of giving you Cosmo's letter to read.

The first time he mounted a horse he was a little afraid, he seemed to be up so very high from the ground, but the horse walked so leisurely down the lane, from the barn to the road, and back again, as if he knew that he had a little boy on his back who would not like him to trot very fast, that Cosmo soon became quite accustomed to his new position.

And the next time, he ventured out on the road a little way. His grandmother, however, was afraid to have him go very far from the house, and so he never rode entirely out of sight.

Once he went with Caleb to the blacksmith's shop to get the horses shod, Cosmo riding Charley, and Caleb, Bessie. This was just after he recovered from his lameness; and when he came back Ettie was standing on the piazza watching for him.

"Wouldn't you like to ride, Ettie?" he screamed as he saw her there. "If grandpapa will lift you up I will hold you on, before me; I saw a little girl ride so, as I was coming along just now."

His grandfather, who was standing by Ettie, laughed as he heard this proposition, and answered for her: "I think it is as much as we can expect of you, Cosmo, if you keep on the horse yourself; but if Caleb will give Ettie a little ride, I will trust her with him."

Caleb, who had just entered the lane with Cosmo, very willingly consented, so Mr. Linton lifted her on the horse and seated her before Caleb, who held her with one arm, while he guided the horse with the other.

"Sit still, Ettie," called Mrs. Linton, as the horses trotted out of the gate, for Cosmo went too; "and don't laugh too loud," she added, as the sound of Ettie's merry laugh came ringing back.

"Ettie might ride alone," said Mr. Linton as he saw how pleased she was; "if she only had a lady's saddle."

"I think we might borrow one from one of the neighbors," replied Mrs. Linton. "There's the widow Barton, her daughters ride sometimes, for I have seen them pass here on horseback."

"So have I," said Mr. Linton, "now you mention it, I remember I saw one of them yesterday. I will send Caleb to borrow it to-morrow."

Just as he said this, the horses came trotting back, with their precious burdens. Cosmo rode on to the stable, but Caleb stopped to leave Ettie. Mr. Linton lifted her off, and while she ran with sparkling eyes and heightened color, to tell her grandmamma how much she had enjoyed her ride, her grandpapa spoke to Caleb about going for the side-saddle.

Caleb said he knew that Mrs. Barton had one, and as it was only about half a mile from there, he proposed to go for it then. But Mr. Linton said it was rather late for Ettie to ride, and it would be better to wait until to-morrow.

Caleb had taken a great fancy to Ettie, she was so gentle and always spoke so civilly to him, and seemed to be so much interested in learning about the farm and he was glad to do any thing for her. She never seemed to mind his laughing at her as he had done that very afternoon, because she had called a field of barley wheat, but said so good-naturedly, "You know, Caleb, I have never been in the country before," that he was ready to do any thing for her, to make up for his laughing at her.

So the next morning early, he was off for the saddle before he commenced his day's work, and by the time Ettie had finished her breakfast, Bessie was waiting for her to mount.

She ran in great glee to borrow a skirt from her grandmamma.

"For you know," said she; "that ladies always have their dresses hang far below their feet when they ride."

Her grandfather lifted her on to the horse, and she presented quite a pretty picture, as she sat perched up there, with the long, black skirt flowing over her feet, and her round straw hat shading her laughing face. Caleb thought so at any rate, as he came to look at her.

"The widow Barton says you may keep the saddle until next week," said he; "for her daughter Mary Jane has gone away somewhere for a visit, and the other one is sick."

Mr. Linton led the horse once up and down the lane, and then Ettie wanted to take the reins in her own hands, so he gave them to her, only walking by the side of the horse.

By this time Cosmo had saddled Charley, for he had learned to do that for himself, and mounting him, had come to be her escort. He begged his grandfather to let them go out in the road together, but to this he would not consent. The most that he would allow her to do was to ride in the lane with Cosmo while he went into the barn to attend to the men who were threshing there.

Cosmo gave Ettie a great many directions; which rein she must pull when she wanted to turn to the right, and which, when she wanted to go to the left, until he confused her so that she could not think which was her right hand, and which was her left. So that when they wanted to turn she pulled the wrong rein, and the horse went up to the fence right under the branches of an apple tree, which overspread the lane.

If Ettie had been a little taller, her head would have been caught in the branches, and she might have been left hanging there; as it was, she had to stoop a little.

"Pull the other rein, Ettie," said Cosmo, "pull the other rein;" but Ettie was a little frightened and couldn't think which rein to pull, so her grandfather who saw the trouble she was in, came to her assistance and turned her horse for her.

Then they rode on very nicely for a while, Ettie remembering when they came to the end of the lane, which rein to pull, in order to turn her horse. Once as she was passing the stable-door, she gave the reins a jerk, and Bessie thought she meant to go in, and was just marching in the door, when Ettie turned her right again.

By the time the ride was finished, Ettie felt quite at ease on the horse, and was eager to try it the next day.

Mr. Linton let the children ride their horses the next time in a pasture-lot which joined the orchard where the swing was, and there they could ride round and round without having to make such short turns as when they rode in the lane.

The horses were very gentle, and seemed to know that they must be unusually so when they had the little folks on their backs, and the children enjoyed their rides more than any of their country amusements; even Whitefoot and Lily were second now, to Bessie and Charley.

But while Cosmo was enjoying his visit so much, his father and mother were very lonely without him. And they began to think it was time for him to come home, for the summer and his vacation were now almost over, and they wanted to see their boy.

Margaret, too, was impatient for his return. She said that if Cosmo did not come home soon, she would have to pick up a boy somewhere to bring home in his place, for she could not stand the quiet of the house any longer. Besides, she had nothing to do; there was no one to put things out of place, and she was afraid she should forget how to darn, or sew on buttons. She forgot that she was always scolding him when he was at home, for tearing his clothes, though she always said more than she meant; but now she was sure that it would do her good to see a large rent once more. She would leave her work any time to go to the window when she heard a boy whistling in the street, it made her think of Cosmo, though to be sure she often told him when he was at home, that his whistling would disturb his grandma.

So it was concluded in the family council that every body wanted Cosmo at home again, and Mr. Linton went to bring him back. For as Ettie was to come too, he did not think it best to leave them both to return alone; besides, he wanted to see his father and mother.

He wrote to say that he was coming, but he did not say what day, so Cosmo was much surprised on awaking one morning to hear his father's voice under the cherry-tree by his window.

"Why, papa!" he exclaimed, as he ran to the window and looked out to make sure that it was indeed his father, "I did not know you were here; when did you come?"

"Why, last night after you had gone to bed. You were sleeping soundly enough, I can tell you, when I saw you, and I hardly knew you; you looked more like a brown country lad, than the pale city boy I sent off on a steamboat a few weeks ago. But come, hurry down, I want to see that celebrated calf of yours, and every thing else that you have to show me."

Cosmo was not long in obeying his father's call, and before breakfast they had visited the orchard to pay their respects to Whitefoot and admire the swing and the see-saw, and had been to the barn and the garden.

As they were returning to the house, Ettie came to meet them, and of course she must show her family of chickens; the kittens had to be left until after breakfast.

Cosmo's father said they must finish all their fun that day, for the next morning they must start for home. So after breakfast they all started for a drive in the large wagon which carried them to church. Ettie and Cosmo, and his father and grandfather all went and even grandmama was persuaded that the house could do without her one morning, and accompanied them. Cosmo was proud to show his father how well he could drive, and Ettie enjoyed telling about the different places which they passed. On their way home they drove down to the mill to say good-by to James and Mattie Ford. It had been quite an event to them to have the little city children come to their quiet neighborhood, and they were sorry to have them go away.

Cosmo's father invited them to come and visit him some time in the city, while Ettie said sorrowfully that she lived so far away

that she supposed they would never come to
see her; however, she hoped to come to her
grandfather's next summer, and then they
would meet again.   And so they parted with
regret on both sides.

That afternoon Mr. Linton had to go to the
pasture-lot, and see Cosmo and Ettie ride.
Then he was persuaded to take a ride himself;
but he was not quite contented to go round
and round the ring, so he trotted off to see
the country, and call on some of his old
friends, leaving Cosmo to help Ettie off from
her horse, and lead Bessie to the stable.

They were to take an early start the next
morning, so breakfast was an hour earlier
than usual, but Cosmo found time to visit
Whitefoot first.

His grandfather found him in the orchard
feeding her and patting her for the last time.

"You feel sorry to leave her, don't you,
my boy?" said he; "but never mind, I will
take good care of her, and when you come

again next summer, you will find her grown
very much."

"I am afraid she will not know me,
though."

"Oh! she won't forget you, no fear of that;
there, see, she wants to assure you of it," said
his grandfather, as Whitefoot rubbed her head
against her young master, as if to say: "How
could you think so ill of me?"

"Good-by, my pretty Whitefoot," said
Cosmo, and he kissed her white face as she
put it up towards him.

Ettie had also been to give her Lily family
their breakfast for the last time, and as she
could not take any of them with her, her
grandmama had consented to let her take a
kitten, to Cosmo's great dismay.

"Why, it will mew all the time on the
boat," said he, as he saw Ettie tying up the
basket in which she had deposited the kitten,
"and it will be nearly frightened to death by
the noise."

"Don't you mind him, Ettie," said her uncle, as she looked imploringly at him; "we will take care of the kitten—you and I, and I don't believe it will trouble any one."

And so the basket containing the kitten was placed on Ettie's trunk while they all went to breakfast.

They were still at the table when the wagon drove to the door. Cosmo insisted upon helping Caleb lift the trunks into the wagon, though if the truth could be told, they would have been in much quicker without his help. One seat had been taken out to make room for them. Then Ettie's grandfather lifted her in, and grandmamma handed her the kitten, who was running round and round in the basket, as if to make the most of the small space to which she was limited.

"You'll get tired enough of her," said Cosmo, as he climbed into the wagon and took his place on the front seat by the side of his grandfather.

"No," said Ettie, "I mean to hold her on

my lap all the time, and she will lie down and go to sleep when we get started; won't you, Kitty?" she added, as she gave the basket a little tap.

Kitty responded by a faint mew, and then, as if she had understood the nature of the promise required of her, she settled herself quietly down on the soft bed of hay provided for her, and was asleep almost before the wagon drove out of the gate.

It was not without many kisses and promises to come again that the children left their kind grandmamma, but as Cosmo looked back as they drove past the house, and saw her still gazing after them with Abby and Sophy, he gave one more parting shout: "Good-by, grandmamma; I will be back again perhaps at Thanksgiving."

Ettie said with a little sigh: "I wish I could say so, but I'm afraid we live too far away to come then."

"I hope you will both come and stay all next summer with us," said her grandfather;

" we shall be very lonely without our children."

"I should think you would be glad to be rid of such noisy little people," said Cosmo's papa, but he smiled when he said it, so every body knew he was only in jest.

He would not have said it at all if he had heard the children's grandmamma, who, after watching the wagon until it was out of sight, declared, as she went into the house, that it seemed as if a gleam of sunshine had gone.

The travellers reached the boat in good time, and received a hearty welcome from the kind captain. Ettie, still carrying the kitten, went with Cosmo and his papa to the upper deck, and as the boat pushed off, waved their farewell to grandpapa, who stood on the wharf to see them go.

"Dear grandpapa," said Cosmo, after they were so far away that they could no longer distinguish any one on the wharf, " it seems but the other day that I was on this very boat looking for him, and now my visit is over and I am going home. I have had a nice time, though, and grandpapa and grandmamma have been very kind to me."

"They have, indeed, my son," said his father, "and I am glad to have you think of it. One of the greatest blessings children like you and Ettie can enjoy is having such wise and tender grandparents as you have, and I hope they may be long spared to you. You should love and revere them next to your own parents. They seem to think no effort too great to make for your happiness."

"Yes," said Ettie, "every day they tried to think of something for our pleasure; and then grandmamma this morning, took all the trouble to get me this basket and tie Kitty in it for me."

Kitty, hearing herself spoken of, thought it was time to wake up from her nap. She was rather anxious besides, to understand what all the puffing and jarring meant that she heard; so she pushed her head against the cover, trying to lift it up, but it was tied down too firmly for that. So Kitty, finding she could not get out in that way, began to mew most piteously, very much to Cosmo's annoyance, and to the amusement of the passengers who happened to be sitting near. They could not tell where the sound came from, until they heard Ettie speaking to Kitty and telling her to be quiet.

"You had better give her something to eat," said a lady who sat near Ettie.

But Ettie was afraid Kitty might get away if she took her out of the basket to give her milk. She, however, lifted up the cover far enough to give her some crumbs of cake, which apparently satisfied her, as she kept quiet afterwards until they reached Cosmo's home when she had a good supper of bread and milk.

If you have ever been away from home for several weeks, you know just how glad Cosmo was to get back again, and his mother welcomed him just as warmly and kissed him just as affectionately as your mother welcomed and kissed you when you came home.

"Now it seems like old times again," said Margaret, as she heard Cosmo running about the house and looking into all the rooms to see if they had changed any.

"But how he has grown!" she exclaimed, as she looked after him as he left the room. "I can not say that I like to see him tanned so much, though."

"Oh! that is no matter," said his mother; "he looks well and robust, and that is all I care for; and he is the same warm-hearted, affectionate boy that he was when he went away, glad to get home again, though he has enjoyed his visit so much."

And now, as this book only proposed to tell of "Cosmo's visit to his Grandfather," and as that visit has ended, it is time the book should end too. Though I know that there are some little readers who would like to know what Cosmo and Ettie did during the week she spent with him after he returned home. But I have no time to tell about that now. Her father promised, when he took her home, that she should come some time and make Cosmo a long visit; and if she does, I will tell you about that, which will be much better.

But was it not hard for Cosmo to go back to school again and study after the pleasant time he had had in the country? I think I hear some boy say.

Why, yes, it was rather hard, and he often found himself wondering what Whitefoot was doing, and thinking of the see-saw and the swing, the brook and the hay-field, when he ought to have been thinking of the capes of North-America or the rivers of Asia.

But his mother told him that the best way in which he could repay his friends who had tried to add to his enjoyment through the summer, was by being more diligent than ever in his duties now. And so when he found his thoughts wandering in this way, he tried to bring them back again to his lessons.

And when his father saw his efforts to do right he said to his mother, "I think that Cosmo's visit to his grandfather has done him good, and if we ever have to go away from home we will take him with us."

And if they ever do, I hope you are interested enough in Cosmo to wish me to tell you all about it.